Give Hope a Chance

A Chance and a Hope
Book Three

SJ McCoy

A Sweet n Steamy Romance

Published by Xenion, Inc

Copyright © 2017 SJ McCoy

Give Hope a Chance Copyright © SJ McCoy 2017

All rights reserved. Except as permitted under the U.S. Copyright Act of 1976, no part of this publication may be reproduced, distributed, or transmitted in any form, or by any means, or stored in a database or retrieval system without prior written consent of the author.

Published by Xenion, Inc.
First Paperback edition 2017
www.sjmccoy.com

This book is a work of fiction. Names, characters, places, and events are figments of the author's imagination, fictitious, or are used fictitiously. Any resemblance to actual events, locales or persons living or dead is coincidental.

Cover Design by Dana Lamothe of Designs by Dana
Editor: Mitzi Pummer Carroll
Proofreader: Aileen Blomberg and Marisa Nichols

ISBN 978-1-946220-26-4

I Hope You Enjoy Reading This!

Well, we finally made it to the conclusion of Chance and Hope's story. I hope you've enjoyed the journey. I certainly have. Chance has been one of my founding characters. He's a big part of the history of Summer Lake, and he helped me to understand the place and the people there. Remington Ranch came into being when I began to wonder what this ranch where he lived in Montana was like. The Remington brothers showed up in answer to my musings about who he worked with and why he'd gone there. It took him a long time to be ready to tell his own story—he's been in my head for over three years now. I hope you've enjoyed getting the chance to see him grow and heal over the course of these three books.

I won't ramble too much; I know you'll want to get on and read—especially since I made you wait so long! ;0) I just wanted to thank you for being here, for reading, and hopefully enjoying these stories. I started writing as a way to escape to a happier place after my son died. I needed a lighter, fluffier place than my own reality, so I went to Summer Lake. Chance has been a thread through all my books—a reminder that grief never leaves us. In writing A Chance and a Hope, I wanted to explore—for myself and for everyone else who lives with the kind of grief that never goes away—the ways we can still have hope and happiness. I hope you'll find a few smiles in here, even alongside the tears. I think that's the way life goes, isn't it? There will always be tears, but we can always find reasons to smile again if we try hard enough.

Anyway, I'll shut up and get out of the way and let you read. I need to get back to writing. I've been invited back to Summer Lake for a wedding ;0)

Take care.

Love,

SJ
oxo

Chapter One

"What time are you leaving?" asked Beau.

Chance looked up at the clock on the wall just inside the barn door. "She's supposed to land at three-thirty, so I'll finish up with this fella and then go take a shower before I head to the airport." He patted Maverick's neck as he finished brushing him down.

Beau smiled. "I guess we won't see much of you this weekend, then?"

Chance shook his head with a grin. "I doubt it."

"How long has she been gone?"

Chance's grin faded. "Almost two weeks." He shrugged. "She wanted to get done sooner, but I guess setting up her business to function without her wasn't as easy as she'd hoped."

"Never mind. At least now she's done it, she shouldn't have to go back again anytime soon."

"I hope not. The theory is that now she's extricated herself from the athletic wear, she'll be free to get on with her life here."

"And she's going to be day trading, is that right?"

"Yup, her dad's going to be teaching her everything he knows."

Beau laughed. "I imagine that'd take a lifetime or two. Seymour Davenport is one smart man."

Chance nodded. "He must be. I don't claim to understand the markets and all the money he makes, but he built his huge empire out of nothing."

"And he's smart enough to know when his daughter's found a good man, and smart enough to want to come home and be part of her life, just in time for grandkids to start coming along."

Chance laughed. "He's got a while before that happens."

"I bet it won't be too long," said Beau with a grin. "You're not getting any younger, Chance. You two need to get married and start making babies already."

Chance pressed his lips together, but it was more to hold in a smile, than an expression of annoyance. "I haven't even asked her yet."

"I know, but you're going to, right?"

"Yeah, I am." Chance couldn't hold the smile in any longer. "And I'm going to do it soon. I don't see the point in wasting too much time. We both know it's what we want."

Beau grinned. "So just get on with it."

"I plan to, just as soon as I come up with something good."

"What kind of something? What do you mean?"

"I mean …" Chance shook his head and shrugged.

"What? What's up?"

Chance rolled his eyes. "I'm embarrassed, is what's up. I thought you guys all went soft when you met the girls. Each one of you started doing weird stuff, stuff that was out of character, but it was kind of sweet. I was fascinated by the effect that meeting the right woman had on you." He reached up and tilted the brim of his hat back so he could look Beau in the eye. "Now I understand it. I'm embarrassed to admit it, but every night since Hope left I've spent hours sitting there trying to dream up the perfect way to ask her to marry me. I want it to be special. I want it to mean something to her, to be a moment that she'll always remember. You know?"

"Aww," Beau shoved his shoulder with a grin. "That might be the sweetest thing I've ever heard you say."

Chance narrowed his eyes at him, but couldn't help smiling back. "A word to the wise?"

"What's that?"

"Don't ever call me sweet again."

Beau laughed. "Or what? You don't scare me anymore; I know you're just a big teddy bear really."

Chance shook his head. "And there I was thinking that you might show some understanding, maybe even try to help me out with an idea or two. You're still an asshole really, aren't you?"

Beau was still grinning. "Yeah, I can still pull off the asshole exterior, even though I'm just as mushy on the inside as you are. You'll learn to hide it again after a while. Are you serious about wanting help, though? I'll brainstorm with you, if you like, but will it be the same if the way you propose is my idea? I thought it had to be something you came up with yourself."

Chance sighed. "Yeah, you're right. It should be. It's just that I'm stumped. Everything I can think of that she might like, isn't something that I'd feel comfortable doing."

"Like what?"

"Like taking her out for a fancy dinner and ..."

"Whoa!" Beau held up a hand. "Not only no, but hell no! That's way too generic, plus it just wouldn't be you. You're asking her to marry you—Chance Malone, broody cowboy, badass, wounded soul, introverted you. You need to come up with something that's as unique as you are."

Chance nodded. "I guess. I was thinking more along the lines of doing something she might enjoy. You know, the fancy restaurants and that kind of thing?"

"Does she really enjoy that, or is it just something that's been a part of her life? The life that she's in so much of a hurry to give up to come here and live in a cabin with you?"

Chance smiled. "Yeah. I guess you're right. I hadn't thought of it like that."

"Well, you need to start thinking that way, bro. You're the man she wants; this is the life she wants. If you're going to do something special, it needs to be born of who you are. That's what will make it special."

"Daddy!" Little Ruby came skipping down the path toward them, with her mom, Corinne, following her.

"Hey, Pumpkin. Are you ready to go?"

"Yes! And yes, I've been good."

Beau smiled at Corinne as she reached them. "Hey, beautiful."

"Hey yourself." She turned to smile at Chance. "Hello, Chance."

Chance watched the two of them as Corinne leaned against Beau briefly and he planted a kiss on her forehead and placed a hand over her stomach. The little hairs on the back of Chance's neck stood up. The way Corinne covered Beau's hand with her own and smiled up at him, Chance just knew it—they were pregnant.

Beau looked up and caught him watching them. He nodded briefly and his eyes shone with happiness and something Chance could only imagine was pride. It made him wonder what that must feel like—to know you were about to be a father. He sucked in a deep breath. He needn't concern himself too much with that just yet. First, he had to figure out how he was going to ask Hope to marry him. He untethered Maverick and led him away through the barn. "I'll leave you guys to it. I need to get going if I'm going to have time for a shower before I leave for the airport."

Corinne smiled at him. "Say hi to Hope for me? And let me know when the two of you want to come over for dinner."

"Thanks, I will."

Beau chuckled. "But it won't be for a while yet, right?"

Chance grinned and shrugged at them as he led Maverick away. It wouldn't. He wanted Hope all to himself for at least the next few days. He couldn't believe how much he'd missed her while she'd been gone. And from their long phone conversations every night, he knew she felt the same way.

~ ~ ~

"Parting is such sweet sorrow." Toby gave Hope a forlorn look when they got out of the car at the airport.

She smiled, but she was feeling a little teary. "We'll see each other soon."

"I know, but it won't be the same, will it?"

Hope sighed and shook her head. "It won't. I hope you're going to come and visit me, and you'll be my first port of call whenever I come back, but you're right, it won't be the same."

Toby nodded sadly. "We had a good run."

She chuckled. "We did, but now we're each moving on to better things. Even if I were staying here, it wouldn't be the same. You spend every spare moment with Sirena these days." She held up a hand when she saw the look on his face. "And that's as it should be. We got each other through when neither of us had anything else going on in our lives, but now you have Sirena, and I have Chance." She stepped forward and hugged him. "And we'll always have each other." There were tears in her eyes when she let go of him and stepped back again. She wasn't surprised to see that his eyes were glistening, too.

"We will. Anything you need, all you have to do is shout. I'll be right there."

Hope smiled. "And the same goes for me. Anything, anything at all, Toby. You promise me, you'll always come to me? If you need an ear or a shoulder or help or advice or …"

Toby laughed. "I promise. And although we're making a big deal out of this goodbye, we both know I'll be bending your ear within a week about something Sirena said or asking you what I should or shouldn't say or do."

"I know, the only thing that's changing is how far apart we'll be. There'll be more miles in between us, but we'll still be as close."

"I hope so. And I'd better be one of the first people you call when Chance pops the question."

She smiled, hoping that would be a call she'd be able to make very soon. "You'll be right up at the top of my list. I promise."

"Good. And say hi to him for me, won't you? I'm sad he's taking you away, but I'm still glad you found him. He's a good man; he's the right man for you."

Hope nodded. "I will, and he is. He's not really taking me away, though. What he's done is given me the chance to go home."

Toby nodded. "How amazing is that? That you go to Oregon and meet a guy who lives in the same place where you grew up? What are the odds? It's a miracle; it must be fate."

Hope chuckled. "Actually, the odds aren't that long when you think about it. We were both there because of Uncle Johnny …"

"Stop!" Toby held up his hand. "Don't spoil it with logical connections. I much prefer to believe that destiny brought the two of you together. I like your Uncle Johnny, but that just doesn't sound quite so romantic."

Hope nodded. "You're right. I'll go with your version instead. Chance and I were just meant to be."

Toby sighed and looked toward the doors where the pilot stood waiting. "I suppose I'd better let you go."

"Yeah." She nodded sadly. "I'd better not keep him waiting or we'll miss our slot. I'll call you when I land, okay?"

"You'd better." Toby put an arm around her shoulders and walked her over to the pilot. "You take care of you, Hopey. Be happy, okay? And if Chance ever screws up and hurts you, he'll have me to answer to."

Hope had to wipe the tears away as she nodded. She knew he meant it. She was so lucky to have him. "Thanks, Toby." She hugged him one last time. "You be happy, too. Sirena had better be good to you."

He nodded. "She is."

As she followed the pilot out through the doors, Hope knew that this chapter of her life was ending. She was sad to leave Toby behind, but he was beginning a new chapter of his own, and there was nothing else she would miss about this part of her life. It was over, and she was ready to step into the future with Chance.

~ ~ ~

Chance pulled into an empty space outside the general aviation building at the Bozeman airport and cut the engine. Instead of getting out of the truck, he sat back a moment. He was early; Hope wasn't due to land for another fifteen minutes. He watched an elderly couple come out of the building and walk toward a waiting SUV. The driver jumped out to greet them while the porter brought their bags. Chance shook his head. Not that long ago he'd felt like he lived in a different universe from people like that. People who traveled in private aircraft, who had drivers and such, were a different species in his mind. At least they had been. His views had started to change when he first met his brother-in-law, Dan. Dan had made millions with his tech company, and his brother, Jack, had a private, well, a corporate jet that he and his partner flew around in. That jet had even come here last year to pick Chance up and get him home in a hurry when his dad had his stroke. Chance shook his head at the memory. For a while there he'd thought he might not make it back to the lake to see his dad one last time. He'd been so grateful to Dan for sending the jet—and even more grateful for the opportunity that trip had given him to rebuild his relationship with his dad before it was too late. Getting to know people who lived that way had showed him that they weren't any different. Hope and her family had shown him that. They might have more money, more things, life might be a little easier for them in some respects, but maybe it was harder for them in other respects.

He started at the sound of his phone ringing and fished it out of his pocket. It was Carter.

"Hey. Is everything okay?"

"It is. Is she there yet? Has she landed? I'll let you go, if she has."

Chance smiled. "No, I'm a few minutes early. What's up?"

"Nothing. You're going to think I'm a big ole dumbass, and you'd be right."

"Don't you go calling my brother a dumbass."

Carter chuckled. "You should reserve judgment till you know why I'm calling."

"Go on, then. I can't talk for long. I want to be in there waiting when she lands."

"I know. It's just that I understand how you're feeling right now. When I heard you were going to pick her up this afternoon, it took me back to when Summer arrived for her three-month stay. I went to pick her up from the airport and I sat outside in the truck a minute, wondering what the future might hold. I just wanted to let you know I'm with you while you're no doubt sitting there feeling the same way."

Chance smiled. "Thanks, Big C. That means more than you know."

"Hey. I just wanted you to know. I'll leave you to it. Be happy."

"Thanks. I'll see you soon."

The line buzzed. Carter had already hung up. Chance kept smiling, even though he had a lump in his throat. If anyone was sweet, it was Carter. He was such a kind, gentle soul—even if he was built more like a bull than a teddy bear. He checked the clock on the dash. Hope was supposed to land in five minutes. He crammed his hat on his head and climbed out of the truck. It was time—time to get started on the rest of his life.

Inside the building he stationed himself by one of the pillars. He had a view of the taxiway from here and should be able to see her plane come in. He grinned when he realized it was already outside. His heart leaped in his chest when he saw she was coming toward the doors on the back of a golf cart. He started toward the doors and then changed his mind. He wanted to watch her. He wanted to see her come in and look around for him. She got down from the cart and chatted for a moment with the kid who was driving it. She always took the time to talk to people, always went out of her way to make people smile. He loved that about her. He smiled to himself as the kid watched her ass as she walked away. Chance couldn't blame him; he watched her ass whenever he got the chance himself.

When she came through the doors she looked around. Her smile faded a little when she didn't spot him immediately. Chance's blood ran cold in his veins and he hurried forward to meet her, deciding as he went that he was going to do everything he could to never disappoint her.

She turned toward him and her smile lit up her face. "Chance!" She hurried to him and flung herself into his arms.

He closed them around her, loving the way she felt, and knowing she was now back where she belonged. "I missed you, honey."

She looked up into his eyes and planted a kiss on his lips. "I missed you more."

He chuckled. "I don't think that's possible."

"Oh, it is. You have no idea."

He hugged her tighter. "Neither do you. All that matters is that you're back now."

She nodded, her blue eyes shining. "I am. I'm back home."

Chance closed his eyes for a moment, wanting to believe that she meant he was her home, but knowing she meant Montana. "Where are your bags? Are they bringing them out?"

She shook her head and looked guilty as hell.

He had to laugh. "What? What are you up to?"

She shrugged. "I wanted to bring a few things back with me, since I'm going to be living here."

"Yeah, I thought you would. So, where are they?"

"I'm having them sent to Oscar's."

Chance frowned. "I thought you were coming to the cabin—to be with me?"

"I am!" She laughed. "Don't worry. I'm not backing out on you; I'm just trying to ease you in. I may have understated a little when I said a few things. I didn't want to scare you silly on my first day back by filling your place up with all my stuff." She winked at him. "I thought I'd lull you into a false sense of security by moving in with just a case full of clothes, and then I'll sneak my stuff into your place little by little."

He laughed and shook his head. "You don't need to do that. You can bring it all, and besides, it's not my place anymore. It's our place." He wanted it to be true, but it didn't feel it. The cabin was the home he'd shared with Mason and Shane. It wasn't a girly house. It wasn't enough for Hope.

She raised an eyebrow, seeming to understand what he was thinking. "I hope it will be, but it'll take time. It won't just suddenly be ours because I walk through the door or move stuff in. It will become ours by the way we live there."

"Yeah. You're right." He narrowed his eyes at her and smiled through pursed lips. "As always."

She laughed. "You really are a fast learner. Can we go home now?"

No matter what he might feel about her belonging at the cabin, he loved the sound of that; they were going home—together.

Chapter Two

When they got to the cabin, Chance turned in his seat to smile at her. "Welcome home, honey."
Hope smiled back. "Thank you. It feels so good to be here. It feels different from before. Before when I came here, I was just visiting you, staying over at your place." She looked through the windshield at the quaint log building. "Now I'm here to stay." She looked back at Chance. "You're stuck with me." The look on his face worried her and she reached out to touch his cheek. "Not really. I was only joking. I know this must be hard for you. If ever you want me to leave you just say so, and I'm gone. I only want you to be with me if it's the right thing for you."
He covered her hand with his own and shook his head slowly. "You're usually good at reading my mind, but you got it wrong that time. If I looked sad, it wasn't because I'm worried about being stuck with you. It's the other way around. I'm worried about you feeling that you're stuck with me. I don't ever want you to feel like your world shrunk because of me. If this," he waved his hand toward the cabin, "if it's not enough for you, don't worry, I know it isn't, I'll get us a better place. But honey, if I'm not enough for you, if you decide one day that

you want more, that you want a bigger life than I can give you, you have to tell me. Don't ever be afraid to tell me if you're done with me. I don't want to hold you down."

Hope's heart raced. "Chance, being with you, being here, living this life, it is a bigger life to me. Life isn't defined by possessions or money or any of that stuff. Life is measured in happiness, and believe me, I couldn't be any happier than I am right now, right here, with you."

He nodded slowly, but she knew he wasn't convinced.

"Chance, please?" She held his gaze. "You don't understand what you mean to me. You don't understand how much being with you has changed my life. And no, I don't mean moving from LA to Montana. I don't even mean that being with you has brought my dad back into my life in a way I didn't think was possible. I mean being with you makes me so happy. I feel alive in a way I haven't since my mom died. I told you that I didn't allow myself to feel, because I didn't know how to not feel too much. You've made me feel again, and it feels so good. I love you, you silly man. I hope you'll learn to understand just how much."

He smiled. "It might take me a while."

She nodded. "I understand. I'll keep doing everything I can to make you understand."

"It might take me the rest of my life."

She nodded. "And I want to be there for every day of it, showing you just how much I love you."

"And I'll be showing you, every day, just how much I love you back." He leaned across and kissed her softly on the lips. "Are you ready? Do you want to go in and get started on the rest of our lives?"

"Yes. I am."

"Okay. Wait there." He got out of the truck and came around to her door. When she opened it, he held his arms out to her with a smile and she wrapped her arms around his neck as he slid his arm under her legs and carried her out.

She pecked his lips and smiled. "I hope you'll always keep up the tradition of carrying me around. Though that first time, you scared the life out of me when I saw you sitting up there on the rocks at the beach."

He smiled back. "I know. I scared you so much you went sprawling."

She shrugged. "I was mortally embarrassed at the time, but I'm so glad I fell. I mean, if I hadn't we might never have gotten to know each other. And even if we'd gotten to talking at the clinic somehow, it wouldn't have been the same." She clung tighter to his neck as he opened the front door. "I love that within five minutes of meeting each other, you'd scooped me up in your arms and carried me away home."

He chuckled. "I couldn't exactly have left you down there on the beach, could I?"

She shook her head. "No. Do you know that when you took me home I was daydreaming about you taking me straight to bed?"

His eyes widened and he looked down at her. "You were?"

She nodded gleefully. "I was. I was so horny. My breasts were rubbing against your chest the whole way back. You felt so strong and manly, and I just wanted you to throw me down on the bed and have your wicked way with me."

He chuckled and closed the door behind him with his foot. "I would never have done that. I'd only known you a couple of minutes." He tightened his grip on her and carried her toward the bedroom. "I've known you a couple of months now, though."

She looked up into his eyes, happy to see the lust in them. "You have, and I'm still hoping you're going to throw me down and ..."

He did exactly as she said, sending a little thrill through her as she landed on the mattress and looked up to see him unbuckling his jeans. "Have my wicked way?" His lips curved up into a smile that she knew by now meant he wanted her badly.

She nodded and pulled her top up and off over her head. His eyes fixed on her breasts as he took his own shirt off then pushed down his jeans and boxers. Hope licked her lips at the sight of him and wriggled around to free her breasts from her bra. They were aching for his touch. He didn't disappoint. He got down on the bed beside her and soon had her out of the bra and her jeans. She sat up to kiss him and he closed one hand around her breast, teasing her nipple with his thumb, while he slid his other hand inside her panties. She gasped as he began to stroke her. She was already wet for him; she'd missed him so much, and it seemed her body had, too. She grasped his shoulders and kissed him deeply, moaning into his mouth as his fingers found their way inside her and began to pump in and out. She was going to come, and there was nothing she could do to stop it. She spread her legs wider and knelt up to give him better access. He dropped his mouth to her neck and nipped her hard, making her scream and bear down on his fingers to take him deeper. He tightened his finger and thumb around her nipple and squeezed sharply, sending shockwaves racing through her. She let her head fall back and began to moan as all the sensations rolled through her. His hand on her breast, his mouth on her neck, and his fingers thrusting in and out of her until it all reached a crescendo and the tension inside her found its release. "Chance!" She screamed as her orgasm tore through her and his talented hands continued their work. "Yes!" She moved with him, her hips rocking frantically as the pleasure crashed through her. "Oh, God, yes!" She moaned when she finally stilled.

He closed his arms around her and hugged her to him for a moment before laying her down. She rolled her eyes at him, knowing what was coming next.

"Don't tell me you can't," he said with a smirk. "Because you know I'm about to prove you wrong."

She smiled. "I know, but I need a minute, before I can give you my best again."

"Your best is right when you think you can't. You'll see."

She chuckled and turned over to crawl away from him. Not because she wanted him to wait, but because she wanted him to take her and make her. She smiled to herself when his arm snaked around her waist and pulled her back to him.

"Where do you think you're going?"

She tried to crawl away again, but his arm tightened around her, pulling her back against him. Thrills raced through her when he planted his knee between hers and spread her legs wider. His coarse fingers stroked her ass and the moan that escaped her lips surprised her. He had both his knees between hers now and his fingers were seeking her heat again. For a moment, she was concerned he was going to make her come that way a second time while he held her from behind. She realized that wasn't his plan when he pulled her back against him and his hot, hard shaft pressed against her ass. His fingers were simply opening her up and guiding him inside her. She closed her eyes and moaned as he moved against her. This was new, and it felt so damned good!

"Are you okay?" His voice was gruff, but still tender.

She nodded, then wondered if he could see that and opened her mouth to reply. The Yes! that came out was an answer to the thrust of his hips that buried his hard shaft deep inside her. He grasped her hips and pulled her back to receive him as he pounded into her over and over and over. She moved with him, taking him deeper and deeper, feeling as though he was filling her mind and soul as well as her body. The little part of her mind that managed to remain somewhat coherent under the barrage of pleasure thought of him as a stallion. He was wild and free and claiming his female, mounting her and … she lost the little grip she'd had on conscious thought and let herself float away on a cloud of pleasure. She was so close to the edge, but she didn't want to go without him. On the next thrust, she felt him tense and she screamed when he let himself go. She felt herself tighten around him, her inner muscles gripping him tight as he spilled his need inside her.

"Damn!" she murmured when they collapsed down onto the sheets. "You really did miss me, huh?"

He chuckled. "I did, and we haven't even started making up for lost time yet. That was just a little welcome home."

She rolled onto her side and planted a kiss on his lips. "I love you, Chance."

"I love you, honey."

~ ~ ~

Chance smiled when he came out onto the back porch. The sight of Hope sitting there sipping her wine made him feel like all was right again in his world. He closed his eyes, and when he opened them he looked up at the big Montana sky and shook his head. He'd sure as hell come a long way since he met her. He stared up into the big blue and implored Chloe to understand. He felt a pang of guilt that Hope made his world right. Some small part of him still clung to the idea that his world could never be right, not without Chloe. The bigger, better part of him had accepted that wasn't true, but it still snuck up on him sometimes—the guilt, the sadness.

Hope looked up and smiled. Her eyes asked if he was okay and he nodded, grateful that she didn't voice the question, and that he didn't have to explain. It wasn't fair to her. He shouldn't spoil the happiness she was feeling, the happiness they were sharing, by talking about Chloe. Not now especially; tonight, was the first night for him and Hope. It was the first night of the rest of their lives together. When he looked at her more closely, he could see Hope had tears in her eyes. He went to her and squatted down in front of her, resting his hands on her knees. "What is it, honey? What's wrong?"

She shook her head. "I don't want to say anything. I don't want to upset you."

He frowned. "The only way you're going to upset me is by not telling me. I'll drive myself nuts wondering what it is. Please?"

She nodded and sucked in a deep breath. "I was just thinking about Chloe."

Chance closed his eyes. "I'm sorry."

"What for?" she looked genuinely puzzled.

"I thought you could tell I was thinking about her."

Hope shook her head rapidly. "I didn't know you were, but I'm glad. I didn't want to bring her up and make you sad."

He shook his head. "What were you thinking?"

She sniffed and blinked away fresh tears. "I was wishing she was still here, that she could see you now. I was talking to her in my head, telling her I'm sorry she missed out on you, but that I promise to do my best to love you and take care of you."

Chance swallowed, but didn't speak. He didn't trust himself yet.

"I feel so bad for her, that she didn't get to live the life she was supposed to, and I feel guilty. I feel guilty that I'm so happy with you, but if she hadn't ... if she were still here, I would never have met you, or you wouldn't even have noticed me if I had. I'm sorry. I shouldn't be bleating to you about how bad I feel. It's a million times worse for you."

He shook his head. "You're not bleating. You're sharing, and I appreciate it. You're braver than I am. I wouldn't have said anything. I came out here feeling so happy about you and me, I was kind of talking to her too. Asking her to understand, wanting her to know that I love you."

Hope nodded and sniffed again. "I'm sorry."

"For what?"

She gave him a weak smile. "I don't even know. I just feel bad. But I only feel bad because things are so good between us. I don't feel bad that they are good. I just ... am I even making sense anymore? I care about Chloe, because she's such an important part of you is, I guess, what it boils down to. I wish I could have known her. I wish she got to feel as happy as I do right now. Part of me feels like I've stolen the happiness that should have been hers."

"No!" Chance gripped her knees tighter. "Don't ever think that. You didn't steal a damned thing. You brought happiness back. You've made me the kind of happy that I didn't think would be possible. Chloe had a huge heart, she loved to see people happy, to make people happy. She'd be pissed at both of us for talking like we are." He brought a hand up to cover his face as his eyes filled with tears. "She'd want us both to be happy and she'd be madder than hell if she knew we were being miserable on her behalf. She'd kick my butt, and she'd kick yours, too, and tell us to get on with it." He nodded. "I know she would."

Hope nodded and smiled through the tears that were streaming down her face. "I believe you. Can I ask you to do something for me?"

"What?"

"Don't ever not talk about her because you think it'll upset me? It won't upset me." She met his gaze. "Okay, maybe sometimes it will, but it won't upset me anywhere near as much as you not sharing how you feel with me. I don't want that kind of distance between us. I know you must think about her a lot, and I'm not asking you to share all of that with me. I just mean I don't want you to not say things because you don't want them to upset me. Okay?"

He nodded. "Okay. I can do that. It'll be easier to do now I don't have to make a decision about whether I should upset you." He gave her a small smile. "I already know you want me to."

She smiled back. "You know what I mean."

"I do. Thanks, honey." He reached up and kissed her lips softly. "You're one amazing woman, you know?"

She smiled. "Thank you."

Chance nodded. He was glad they'd had that conversation, but he wanted to move on from it. They'd said what they needed to. "What do you want to do with what's left of the evening? I wasn't sure how tired you'd be after your trip."

"I'm fine. It's not a very long flight. Do you have any ideas? Do you want to go out or something?"

"Out for a walk maybe, or a ride if you feel up to it." He frowned. "Unless you want to go out out. We could go for dinner at Chico or a drink. Or there's the Lodge." Maybe the fancy restaurant at the lodge would be more to her liking. They hadn't been there yet, and it was where her kind of people liked to eat. Cassidy loved it.

Hope shook her head at him. "Would you relax? I live here now. You don't have to figure out where to take me and how to entertain me, and you certainly don't need to start going to places you don't even like, just for me."

He raised an eyebrow, as if he didn't know exactly what she was talking about.

She laughed. "I do like the Lodge, or at least I used to, it's been a long time, but if it's anything like it used to be then I'm sure you don't like it and I can go there with the girls. Like the hotel at Mammoth."

He smiled. "Okay, fair enough. I'm not going to argue with you on that one."

"I didn't think you would. Do you feel like going for a walk? I'd love to go down by the river."

"Sure. That'd be nice. We can stop and say hi to the horses on the way, if you like?"

"I'd like that a lot. I want to see about getting a horse of my own now I'm going to be here. Do you think they'll let me board one at the barn?"

Chance made a face. "Of course. We all have our horses there. The girls each have their own now, too. We need to start looking for one for you."

Hope gave him a weird smile, as though she had some kind of secret.

"What? Have you already found one or something?"

She shrugged. "Maybe. Maybe not. We don't need to worry about that right now, do we? Let's just go for our walk and say hi to the horses."

"Okay." He got to his feet and offered her his hand. "Anything you say."

She waggled her eyebrows at him. "I'll remind you of that when we get back."

"Please do, I'd be happy to oblige."

Chapter Three

Hope opened her eyes. The morning light streaming in through the window was already bright. She looked at Chance, who slept on beside her, and then at the clock on the nightstand. It was almost seven. He was going to be late. She leaned over and kissed the tip of his nose.
He opened his eyes and smiled. "G'morning."
"You might not think it's so good when you hear that it's seven o'clock already. You'd better get up. I'll go and put the coffee on."
He shook his head and his smile grew wider. "I'm not going to be late, because I'm not working until lunchtime today. I arranged for the guys to cover for me so that we could take our time this morning. I was going to take the whole day, and I still can if you want, but I thought you'd probably want to head up to see your dad."
Hope grinned. "That's perfect! I planned to see him this afternoon, but I didn't expect you to be free this morning."
Chance sat up and leaned back against the headboard. "I missed you. I wanted us to get a little bit of time together before I have to get back to work."

"Thank you. I know it's not easy for you to take much time off."

"It isn't, but it's not impossible. Do you still want to go to Summer Lake? I promised I'd take you, and I can get a few days soon."

"I'd love to, but not if it's a problem for you. We can wait until a better time, if you prefer?"

He shook his head with a smile. "I don't want to wait. Missy's threatening to come up here if I don't take you down there soon, and to say Dad and Alice are eager to see you again would be an understatement. I was hoping you'd say yes, because I need to get them all off my back."

Hope laughed. "Then let's go as soon as you can take the time off."

"What about your dad? Don't you need to get started with him? He's been here waiting for you to come back so he can start teaching you about day trading."

"I'll check with him this afternoon, but from what he's said, he's not exactly just hanging around waiting for me. He's getting on with business as usual, and he's doing a lot of soul-searching. Coming back here and especially staying in the house has made him take stock and start thinking about his life and how he wants to live the rest of it."

"In a good way?"

"The best way. He's finally prepared to deal with his grief and open up to the possibility of really living again, instead of just existing and hiding in his work."

Chance nodded. "Who would ever have thought that he and I would have so much in common?"

Hope smiled. "They say women are attracted to men who remind them of their father. I see so much in you that reminds me of him. Not just grief and the way it affected you, but you both have such a strong work ethic, you're both loyal, and honest to a fault …"

"And what else?"

She laughed. "And broody."

Chance shrugged. "I won't deny that. I don't mean to be broody, I just prefer to think than to talk most of the time, but I have been told a time or two that I come off as broody."

"Don't you worry about it. Broody is sexy."

"It is?"

"It is, or at least it can be when it's not overdone."

He smiled. "Good to know."

"Anyway, Mr. Broody, what do you want to do this morning? I don't want to waste it in bed."

He raised his eyebrows. "You think time spent in bed with me is time wasted?"

"It is if all we're doing is talking."

He slid back down under the covers and drew her with him, pulling the sheet up over their heads and rolling her onto her back. "I told you, I'm not big on talking." As his mouth came down on hers, Hope wrapped her arms around him, loving the feel of his lean hard body against hers. Any time she spent with him was far from wasted—he was the best time of her life.

When they were both showered they took their coffee outside to sit on the back porch. Hope raised her mug to him. "I was so worried about what I was going to do with myself when I moved here, and yet now I'm here that seems silly."

"Why, what do you mean?"

She smiled. "I mean that now I'm here I could quite happily spend my days just sitting out here on the porch, watching the clouds go by. I could cook for us in the afternoons and go riding and hiking and spend time visiting with my dad and Monique and all the girls." She looked at him, wondering if he'd think she was lazy or aimless.

He smiled. "If that's what you want to do, then you should do it. It's not like you have to work, is it?"

She shook her head. She wasn't sure if that was encouragement or if it was a dig at the difference in their financial situations. She smiled brightly, wanting to leave the subject behind. "I kind of do have to. I'm all loved up and relaxed right now, but I'd be climbing the walls within a couple of days if I didn't have anything to do. If I know my dad, I'll have more than enough to keep me busy once we get started. He's a hard task master."

Chance looked concerned. "Are you going to be okay with that?"

"I am. I'm looking forward to it. He is tough, but he's fair and supportive. He demands the best of everyone and he knows how to bring it out of them." She nodded to herself. She'd known that about him all her adult life, but it had never occurred to her before to turn to him, to ask him to help her bring out the best of herself.

Chance's phone rang and he pulled it out of his pocket with a grimace which turned into a smile when he looked at the display. "It's Missy. Do you want to talk about when we're going to visit, or do you want me to put her off till we figure it out for ourselves?"

"Let's talk to her about it, can we? Let's see what will work."

Chance nodded as he answered. "Hey, Miss. What's up?"

Hope had to smile at the look on his face as he listened to whatever Missy was saying.

"Hang on, I'm going to put you on speaker. It'll be easier that way. No, I am not handing you over to her. I need to at least hear what's going on. If I let the two of you cut me out of the loop, I'll stand as much chance as a snowball in hell." He hit the speaker button and laid his phone down on the table. "She wants to talk to you," he told Hope with a rueful smile.

"Hi, Hope! How are you?" Missy's voice rang out.

"I'm doing great thanks. How are you?"

"I'll be doing better when you get that brother of mine to bring you down here for a visit. If he doesn't do it soon, I'm going to have to come up there and I hate to fly."

Hope chuckled. "We were just talking about it this morning. I had to go back to LA for a couple of weeks, but now I've got everything sorted, and I'd love to come see you. We just need to work out when Chance can take off work."

Missy laughed. "Well, if he takes too long, you come by yourself. It'd be nice to see him, but you must know it's you we really want to see. Dad doesn't stop talking about you. He's usually a bit of a grumpy bear, but he gets all chatty and smiley when your name comes up."

Hope smiled at Chance. "I adore him, and Alice too. I didn't get to know them too well; we weren't in Oregon too long, but I love them."

"They love you, too. And I have to say, I'm glad Chance finally got his head out of his ass. I thought he'd blown it when he left Oregon. He can be a bit dumb sometimes, but it's only because he's such a guy. He can't help it."

Hope chuckled at the way Chance blew out a sigh and shook his head. "I'm sitting right here; remember, Miss? I can hear everything."

Missy's laughter echoed down the line. "And? I'm not saying anything we don't already know, am I?"

Chance rolled his eyes and shrugged his resignation.

"We hit a bit of a bump in the road there, but we got past it."

Hope didn't want either one of them to think she was taking sides. She'd gang up on Chance with Missy about the fun stuff, but when it came to anything serious, she wasn't going to pick on him just to get on his sister's good side.

"Yeah, joking aside, Chancey, I'm so happy you got past it and found your way back to each other."

Hope had to bite back a laugh at the sight of him covering his face with his hand.

"So, when do you think you might find your way down here?"

"How about next weekend?" Chance raised an eyebrow at Hope and she nodded; that sounded good to her. As far as she was concerned, the sooner the better. She wanted to go and see his family, and she also wanted to get back and get settled into her new life here.

"Really? You can come that soon? That'd be wonderful!"

"I'll need to make sure it works with the guys, but I think it should. How about I give you a quick call tonight and let you know? I'm off this morning and the plan was to spend it with Hope, not on the phone with you."

Missy laughed. "Why didn't you say so? I'm gone! I didn't expect you to even pick up, I was just going to leave you a message."

Chance laughed. "Damn! It's my own fault for picking up then."

"It is! Don't blame me. Okay, you two have a great day and I'll see you soon."

"Bye, Missy," called Hope.

"Talk to you later," said Chance. He shook his head at Hope when he hung up. "I told you she's a piece of work."

"She seems lovely, and you don't fool me, I can tell you adore her."

Chance nodded reluctantly. "She is pretty awesome really. She's not had it easy, but she's a feisty little madam. She doesn't let anyone or anything stop her."

"I can't wait to meet her."

"Well, you won't have long to wait now. I'll check with Mason and the guys, but we should be fine for this weekend."

Hope nodded. "How do you normally get down there?" She'd been assuming they'd take her plane, but it occurred to her that he might have other plans, and she didn't want to ride roughshod over them.

"I usually drive, but it makes for a long trip. It takes a couple of days to get there and the same coming back. I was thinking we might fly this time. There's a little commercial airport about an hour away from the lake."

Hope decided to ask. She didn't want to tiptoe around. "Do you want to take my plane? It'll be a lot quicker and easier. Is there a local airport nearer to Summer Lake?"

"Yeah, there's one right there just outside of town." She watched his lips press together as he looked away. She hoped she hadn't offended him, but if she had then they were going to need to talk about it. It'd be crazy not to use the jet. He looked back at her and smiled; it was a forced smile, but at least it was there. "Sorry, honey. It's going to take me a while to get over this damned pride of mine. Yes, we should take your plane. It'd be pretty dumb of me to say no, huh?"

She smiled. "I'm not going to agree with that last statement."

He chuckled. "Thank you."

After Chance had left for work, Hope wandered around the cabin. She really did love the place, even if it was smaller than she was used to. She'd get used to it. All that really mattered was that she was here with Chance. At some point, they'd build a place. She knew her dad liked the idea of them building on the part of Chance's land that was closest to his own. She hadn't asked what was happening about the joint ranch idea. It wasn't because she wasn't interested—more because she wanted to stay out of it. She wanted her dad and Chance to be free to talk to each other, for them each to do what was best for them without her being in the middle of it all. Chance hadn't mentioned it since she'd got back last night, but then they'd had plenty of other things to talk about—and to do. Perhaps her dad would say something when she saw him this afternoon. She picked up the keys to the Land Rover, deciding she may as well head up there now.

She smiled when she spotted Shane standing out by the side of the driveway near the guest ranch. He waved and she pulled over.

"Hey, Miss Hope. I'm glad to see you back."

"Thanks, Shane. It's good to be back. Now I just have to get on with setting my life up."

Shane nodded. "Cassidy told me you're going to be working with your dad."

"I am, that's where I'm going right now."

"Oh, don't let me hold you up then."

"No, problem. It's good to see you."

"You too. I thought you were home the other day when I saw the Land Rover parked at the cabin."

"No, I only got in yesterday afternoon. Uncle Johnny and Aunt June dropped this off for me so I'd have something to drive until I buy my own."

Shane nodded. "When you go car shopping, make sure you get something practical."

Hope raised an eyebrow.

Shane grinned. "Sorry, I'm sure you're quite sensible, and, of course, you'll get whatever you want. You just reminded me of Cassidy. The first winter she spent out here, she had a VW Bug. Let's just say it wasn't ideal for the weather or the terrain."

Hope laughed. "I don't imagine it was, but I'm sure she loved it."

Shane chuckled. "She did. I wasn't so keen on it. Can you imagine trying to fit me into the passenger seat?"

Hope really couldn't. Shane was a big guy; he had to be about six feet four. She shook her head. "I hope she's got something bigger now?"

"Yup. I made sure of it."

Hope smiled wondering how that had gone down. Cassidy didn't strike her as a woman who would meekly do what her man suggested.

Shane laughed. "I bought it for her as a gift so she wouldn't be able to argue."

"Ah, wise move. I was thinking of getting myself a Land Rover like this one. Do you think that would be suitable?"

Shane cocked his head to one side. "I don't see why not." He met her gaze with a smirk. "Although I know a certain cowboy who likes all his vehicles to be American made, just like him."

Hope nodded. "Thanks for the tip."

"Hey, I'm not trying to tell you what to do, I know better than that."

"I'm sure you do. And I'm not saying I'll take your advice, but I'm grateful for the information."

Shane laughed. "I can see why Cassidy thinks so much of you, you're a pair together, aren't you?"

"It seems we do have a lot in common."

Shane turned at the sound of voices coming from the lodge. "I'd better get back and see what my guests are up to. Nice talking to you. I'll see you around."

"Okay, see you, Shane."

As she drove up the valley, Hope smiled to herself. There were strong independent women living out here. Women she hoped would become her friends. A little shiver ran down her spine. If she and Chance got married, they'd be her family. She had a feeling that each of the Remington men had had to reevaluate their beliefs about traditional male and female roles. It might be hard for them, but they were adjusting. She knew Chance was struggling, as their conversation about the plane this morning had proved, but she hoped he'd be able to adjust as well as it seemed Shane had.

When she got to the Davenport Ranch she brought the car to a stop in front of Uncle Johnny's house. Aunt June opened the front door and came trotting down the steps to greet her.

"Hopey! It's so good to see you back. How are you? How was your trip?"

"It was good, thanks. I'm glad it's done with. I shouldn't have to go back again for a while now."

"That's good, dear. And are you here to see your father?"

Hope nodded. "Is he up at the house?"

Aunt June smiled. "He is. I'm proud of him. I think he's ready to start living again, and it's all down to you. He's finally opening up again."

Hope smiled. "It's hard to believe the way things are working out, isn't it? Who would ever have guessed that we'd both come back here—and be happy."

"Not me, that's for sure. I won't keep you, if you're on your way to see him. I know he's been eager for you to get back so the two of you can get to work. Don't let him work you too hard and take over, will you?"

"I won't." Hope was a little concerned that once they got to work, she and her dad might get carried away and end up working long hours. It was a trait they shared that once they got into something, they gave it their all. She wondered if she should delay starting until she and Chance returned from Summer Lake. She smiled at Aunt June. "I'll see you later."

"Yes, stop in when you're finished, if you have time, but don't worry if you don't. I love that we're all here now and we can see you any time. I just wish the boys would come back, too."

Hope smiled. "I don't think that's very likely, do you?"

Aunt June laughed. "I think hell might freeze over first, but you never know. I'm a momma, I'll never stop wanting my boys back. And I know your father is waiting to get you back. You'd better go, before I make you late."

Chapter Four

Chance was in the yard outside the barn. He was about to get on Maverick and head out, but he turned at the sound of Dave's voice and smiled.
"How's it going, son?"
"Everything's great. She got back yesterday afternoon and I took this morning off."
Dave smiled. "I'm glad to hear it. I thought it was odd to see you in the barn at lunchtime. So, I used it as an excuse to come say hello. I was worried there might be a problem."
"No problems that I know of, but I haven't been out there yet today. I'm going to check on them now."
"They'll be fine. I know it. You're like me. You're going to have to learn to step back a bit, trust your men to take care of the herd while you take care of your family."
Chance met his gaze and nodded.
"Speaking of your family. How's your dad doing?"
"Better." He always felt a little awkward talking to Dave about his dad. He was loyal to them both, even though that seemed to be a contradiction.
"Good. You should get down there and see him sometime soon."
"We're thinking of going this weekend. He and Alice both want to see Hope again, and Missy can't wait to meet her."

Dave nodded. "I look forward to the day I get to meet them."
Chance sucked in a deep breath and nodded. Part of him looked forward to that day, too. Another part of him didn't relish the idea at all. He'd love to bring Dave and his dad together and he'd love Missy to meet the guys and their wives, but something about bringing his two separate worlds together felt overwhelming.

"I used to think that day would never come," said Dave, "but now I believe it will."

"Why's that?"

Dave smirked. "It'll be your wedding day."

Chance swallowed and nodded again. That hadn't occurred to him, but it was true. He could hardly get married without his dad and Dave being there, or the brothers and his sister, and ... he shook his head. It really was overwhelming.

"I'm not wrong in thinking that you're going to have one of those in the not-too-distant future, am I?"

"I don't think so. I mean. I hope that's the way it's going to work out. It's not marrying Hope that's got me worried; it's the thought of having all of you guys and all my Summer Lake family in the same place at the same time."

Dave smiled. "It must be a strange idea to you, but I like it."

"Why?"

"Because ..." Dave shrugged. "I dunno, maybe I'm getting old, you can call me a sentimental old fool, but to me it'll be like making you whole again. Bringing the two halves of your world and your life together, making them one." He shrugged again.

Chance nodded and blinked rapidly. What Dave said made a lot of sense, but it also made his eyes leak a little too. "I guess we'll just cross that puddle when it rains, huh?"

Dave smiled. "I guess we will. In the meantime, let's get back onto safer ground. Where are you up to on the contract Seymour sent over?"

Chance shook his head. "I've been meaning to come talk to you about that."

"Why? Is there a problem?"

"You've read it, right?"

Dave nodded.

"Then you know what's in it."

"And you have a problem with what's in it?"

"Not for myself, no. He's practically handing me the keys to the kingdom and screwing himself over into the bargain."

"I don't see how he's screwing himself over."

"I guess he's not, but the contract favors me over him. I didn't think he'd do that. I thought there would be sneaky clauses in there to trip me up or close me out."

Dave shook his head. "He's trying to do what's best for you and for Hope. He's protecting her, too. You did see that?"

"Of course. The temporary agreement will become permanent if and when Hope marries me, and it will end if we ever break up. She'd get everything back if that ever happened."

Dave nodded. "It's a kind of prenup, I guess."

"Yeah, except it feels more like it's some kind of weird dowry. If I marry Hope I get all these cattle and all the land and everything. It's weird."

"I honestly believe he's trying to do right by you."

"So do I. It just surprises me."

"It shouldn't. Seymour's a father who wants to do right by his daughter and the man she loves. It doesn't hurt that he likes what he sees in you and has a great deal of respect for you."

"He said that?"

Dave smiled. "He did, repeatedly."

Chance smiled in spite of himself. It was important to him that Hope's father should see him as a good man, as someone he could respect, not just some deadbeat his daughter had picked up and who needed to be managed.

Dave looked up at the sound of voices approaching the barn. "Uh-oh, I think that's Shane's guests on their way out for their afternoon ride. I'm going to skedaddle before they get here. They seem to think I'm as old as the West itself, and once they start asking questions I get stuck with them for hours."

Chance chuckled. "Okay, I'm going to get out of here too. See you later."

Dave tipped his hat and set off at a fair trot back to the cottage.

~ ~ ~

Hope pulled up in front of the house and stared up at it for a moment before she got out of the Land Rover. "I wish you were still here, Mom," she whispered. She closed her eyes for a moment and pictured her mom standing smiling at the top of the stairs outside the front door. She wished she could run up those stairs and hug her. She drew in a deep breath and then slowly blew it out, then smiled. "But I know you're still with me."

She got out and had to blink away the tears when she looked up and saw her dad standing at the top of the stairs smiling, just as she'd imagined her mom doing. Her mom was gone, but her dad was still here, and the two of them were about to embark on a new chapter of their lives, a new chapter of their relationship with each other.

"Come on up," he called. "I've missed you."

"I've missed you too, Dad." When she reached him, she didn't hesitate to go straight to him and hug him. He hugged her back and dropped a kiss on the top of her head. He used to do that when she was small, when her mom was still alive, but she didn't remember him doing it since they'd moved away from this house. "It's so good to be back." She didn't just mean back in Montana; she meant back at a place where hugging each other felt good and genuine.

"It's good to have you back." He smiled and echoed her thoughts. "Back in this house, back in my arms, back in my life."

She nodded. They'd never left each other's lives, but the distance between them for the last twenty years had been more than miles. "This feels like a whole new beginning, doesn't it? We get to leave behind the cold years."

He chuckled. "Is that how you think of it? The cold years?"

She shrugged. "I didn't, not until the words came out of my mouth. But yeah, since Mom died, there was no warmth between us, was there? Now there is, and it feels so good."

"It does." He kept his arm around her shoulders and led her inside. "I'm sorry that I had no warmth to give you. I feel like I was frozen inside." She looked up into his eyes and he smiled. "Now I feel like I'm starting to defrost."

She smiled back. "I like the sound of that."

"I like it, too. I just hope I don't dissolve into a puddle."

She chuckled. "I don't think you'd manage that if you wanted to."

"Probably not. Do you want to come sit outside with me? I thought we could catch up before we start talking about work."

"That sounds good to me."

They sat outside on the deck and sipped the lemonade he had ready for them.

"That tastes so good," said Hope. "Where did you get it?"

She'd never seen him look quite so proud of himself. "I made it."

"You did?!" She couldn't keep the surprise out of her voice.

He chuckled. "I'm not entirely hopeless."

"Sorry, I know, but you're not entirely domesticated either, are you?"

"No, but I'm working on it. You probably won't believe it, but I baked some cookies too."

Hope laughed. She couldn't remember ever seeing her dad bake. "You did? Why?"

He shrugged. "I like cookies."

"You've always liked cookies, I know that, but you've never baked them before."

He nodded; his smile was tinged with sadness. "I spent some time in your mom's sewing room."

Hope pressed her lips together. In all the years since her mom had died, she'd probably been in her mom's sewing room less than half a dozen times. She didn't think her dad ever went in there.

"I needed to. It seems the time has come to do a lot of things I've been avoiding." He nodded to himself. "It was hard, but there was something good about it, too. It made me feel like she's close. She's still here, and she wants me to be happy. I went through her things, they brought back so many memories. I found her little recipe book." He waved his hand at the jug of lemonade. "It took me back to all the times she stood in the kitchen making lemonade. I baked the cookies because it was a recipe she made up especially for me. Normally you get oatmeal or chocolate chip. I like both so much that she started baking oatmeal with chocolate chips in for me." He stared out at the mountains with a sad smile. "She thought I was crazy, but she loved me."

Hope had to blink away the tears. She remembered the lemonade now he'd told her, but she didn't remember the special cookies. Hearing about them gave her a different view of her parents' relationship. She wasn't a little girl anymore.

She was a grown woman, with a relationship of her own, with a man she loved. Thinking of her mom and dad as being just like her and Chance gave her new insight. It made her heart hurt even more for her dad and for the love he'd lost. She reached across the table and squeezed his hand. "I'm sorry, Dad."

He squeezed back and then visibly pulled himself together. "I'm sorry, too. I lost my way for far too many years, but coming back here, coming home, is helping me find my way again."

"I'm glad. I feel the same way."

He nodded. "I guess we have Chance to thank for it. If it weren't for him, neither of us would be here. How is he?"

She smiled. "He's doing great. He took this morning off to spend with me, but he's back out on the range this afternoon."

"Good. I hope he's going to have an even bigger herd to keep him busy soon."

Hope smiled. She didn't want to comment, because she didn't know what to say.

"And you're going to be busy, too." He raised an eyebrow. "If you're still interested in learning about day trading?"

"I am! I'm excited to get started. There is one thing I want to run by you first, though."

"What's that?"

"Chance and I are planning to visit Summer Lake this weekend. We'll be gone for a few days to see his family. Do you think we should get started before I go, or would it be better to wait until I come back?"

"Whichever you prefer. We can wait if you want?"

She shrugged. "I don't know. I want to get started right now, but I know what you're like, and I take after you. Once we get started on something we find it hard to break off."

"It's only a few days, isn't it?"

She nodded.

"Then how about we spend this week giving you an overview? I'll teach you the big picture before we dive in. Then you'll have time to digest the basics while you're away, and when you come back we can get down to business. Unless you'd rather wait? I don't want to force you to start if you're not ready."

"No. I'd much sooner get started."

"Right now?" he asked with a smile.

"Well, I was hoping you might start telling me what you can while we're sitting here drinking Mom's lemonade." She didn't know what made her say that, but it felt right. It felt like saying they were back together again, and that her mom was here with them. The way he nodded told her that it sounded right to her dad too.

"Okay, then. Let's get started." He raised his glass. "Here's to a new beginning."

She touched her glass against his. "New beginnings."

The rest of the afternoon flew by as he told her the basics of day trading. She found it fascinating and loved seeing her dad so animated. It was clear that anything to do with the markets was a true passion for him. It was also clear that he was so successful because he didn't think like most people. It seemed every detail he explained to her, he first told her what was accepted wisdom. Then he proceeded to highlight the pitfalls and to tell her his alternative strategies and the reasoning behind them. Hope loved this new insight into him and his mind. She felt as though she was getting to know him as a contemporary for the first time. This man talking to her wasn't trying to be her father; he was just a man sharing his knowledge and his passion for his work with someone who was interested to learn from him. It felt good.

When he reached a logical breaking point, he looked up at the clock on the wall. "I'm sorry. I had no idea of the time. It's almost six. Do you need to get home?"

Hope shook her head. Chance would be finishing work soon, but she didn't want to leave her dad just yet. "I don't want to go," she said with a smile. "I'll just text Chance and let him know where I am."

"You go if you want to, Hopey. I don't mind. We can carry on tomorrow. Don't you want to be there when he gets home?"

She smiled and shook her head. "I kind of do, but I don't want to set myself up to be the little woman who's there waiting at the door when he gets back. That's not my style and he wouldn't expect it."

Her dad nodded. "Okay, but don't push your independence just to make a point, will you? The two of you are going to become a team, and that means considering each other in all things."

"I know." She smiled. "Maybe I should get going."

"I think so. You can come tomorrow, if you want, but if you need to get ready for your trip, you do that."

"I'll be here, don't worry about that. I did want to ask you something, though. When we talked about Chance being from Summer Lake, you said you knew the place. How? It seems to be the kind of small town I wouldn't have thought you'd even heard of."

"In the normal course of things, I'm sure I never would have heard of it, but a friend of your mom's moved there a long time ago." He nodded, seeming lost in his memories for a moment. "Anne, she was your mom's best friend in college. She was a very talented painter. She met another painter and the two of them did what few artists manage and became successful commercially. They lived in Denver for a little while, but when they were expecting their first child they moved to Summer Lake. They wanted their child to grow up in a small town. We visited them a couple of times. It was a quaint little place, the town itself wasn't anything special, but it had a feel to it." He nodded. "It was a good place. Anne wanted me to move there after your mom died. She thought it would do you good to grow up in a place like that. Maybe she was right. Maybe I should have." He shrugged. "Who knows what it's like now. I lost touch with her and Graham years ago. It hurt too much to talk to them."

Hope nodded. Somehow it helped her to know that he'd closed himself off from her mom's friends—that she hadn't been the only one he'd rejected in his grief.

"I could look them up for you, if you want? Find out if they're still there. If they are I can give you their information and you can choose when you're there if you want to contact them or not."

Hope thought about it. Judging by the way she'd felt when she met Monique, perhaps it would be good to meet her mom's friend, but then that wasn't the point of the visit.

"I'll see what I can dig up, they may not even be there anymore. Their son was doing well for himself in New York; they may have moved closer to him."

"Thanks."

He touched her hand. "I don't know any more than you do if it's something that will help you. I just want to make it a possibility for you if you want to."

She got up and went to wrap her arms around his neck. "Thanks, Dad. I love you."

"I love you, too, Hopey."

Chapter Five

Chance peered out the window as the plane touched down. The first time he'd ever flown in a private plane had been last year when Dan had sent a jet to get him after his dad's stroke. He'd flown in it a handful of times since then—to go to Missy's wedding in Vegas and when he'd gone with his dad to Oregon. It was hard to believe, but he was used to it now. He was glad this wasn't the first time. He felt uncomfortable enough that this was Hope's jet, at least he wasn't a total novice in how it all worked.
She smiled over at him. "I'm excited, but I'm nervous, too."
"You've got nothing to be nervous about. Dad and Alice already love you, and when it comes to Miss, I think I'm the one who should be nervous. I don't think I'll stand a chance once the two of you join forces."
She laughed. "You're probably right there. And she's coming to pick us up?"
He nodded. "She and Dan are coming. You'll like him. He doesn't say too much, but when he does, it's always worth listening."
"He sounds like my cousin Reid."
"He sounds like Oscar in some ways, too. At least, the genius bit, he's no playboy. He's not even a partier or anything, but he's damned smart."

Hope nodded, looking more thoughtful now. "Do you plan to see anyone else while we're here?"

He nodded slowly. "I think so. I'm not sure yet." He'd called Renée a couple of days ago to tell her they were coming. She knew about Hope and claimed to be happy for him. Her husband, Gabe, had gone over the contract Seymour had drawn up for the ranch. But still, it felt weird to be bringing Hope here. It felt wrong of him to ask Renée to accept her. Hope wasn't Chloe, and Chloe had been Renée's sister. Was it fair of him to ask her to accept another woman in her place? He didn't want to talk about all that right now though. Not when they'd be seeing Missy and Dan in just a few minutes. "I told you about the whole gang of friends who live back here now. I'll have to ask Miss if they're all getting together at any point over the weekend. If they are, we could maybe drop in for a little while."

Hope smiled. "That'd be fun. Do you usually do that when you come back?"

He shrugged. "Sometimes." How could he explain that he saw the gang if Missy forced him into going along? He usually bumped into most of them around town when he came, but seeing them individually was a whole lot easier for him than having to go sit at the Boathouse with a dozen people all talking and asking questions—even if they were his friends.

"Let me guess, you usually skulk around the edges of town, and this time I'm landing you right in the middle of everything?"

He had to smile. "Yeah, pretty much."

"We don't have to do any of it, if you don't want to. We can just see your dad and Alice and Missy and Dan. I hope I'll get to meet her son, Scot, too, but other than that, I don't want you to have to do anything that makes you uncomfortable. You can keep a low profile if that's easier."

He nodded. "Thanks, honey. It would be easier, but easier isn't always better, is it? We're both trying to skirt around it, but part of bringing you here is to keep pushing myself. I've found ways to deal with so many things since we met. Now I need to see if I can deal with you being here. With me being with you here." He sighed. "You know what I mean. This place is Chloe's home. It was supposed to be our home."

"I know. That's why I'm saying you don't have to do anything that makes you uncomfortable. Maybe it's too soon. Maybe it will never be right for me to be here. I get it."

He shook his head. "I know you do, but I need to move through it, move past it. It's not as though Chloe minds you being here. It's me. I need to break down all the walls I built up in my head and around my heart. It's going to be uncomfortable, but that's okay. Change is always uncomfortable, but without change, there can't be any growth. And I need to grow. I need to ..."

The plane came to a halt and the pilot's voice came through the speakers in the cabin. "Welcome to Summer Lake. I'll be right through to open the doors and there's a golf cart waiting for you on the tarmac. That will take you to the FBO building where they tell me your friends are waiting to collect you."

Hope pressed a button in the arm of her seat. "Thanks, Randy. Are you all set for your stay here?"

The pilot didn't reply, instead appearing in the doorway from the cockpit a moment later. "Sorry, I thought it was easier to come talk to you. I am, thanks, Hope. Apparently, there's a little resort in town. I have a room there and a rental car. It seems like a great little town, I'm looking forward to the weekend, thanks." His smile faded. "But of course, I'll be on standby whenever you need me."

Hope smiled. "How about you consider yourself off call until Sunday afternoon? If anything crops up in the meantime, we'll find another way out of here. That way you can really relax and enjoy yourself."

He started to shake his head, but Hope fixed him with a questioning look. "Please?"

He smiled. "Okay, then, if you insist, but I'm going to find one of the local pilots and see if they can stand by, just in case. I hate the idea of you having an emergency and not being able to get out of here."

"Okay, if that's what it'll take before you'll relax, then do it."

Once they were on the golf cart heading toward the FBO building Chance turned to Hope. "What was that all about with Randy? Why can't he just take the weekend off and still be on call if you need him?"

Hope smiled. "Because flying is different from most other jobs in that respect. When he's on standby, he has to be ready to be at the airport and in the air within an hour. That means he can't go too far and he can't really relax at all. It also means he can't have a drink all weekend. They call it eight hours from bottle to throttle. Which is fine, if you go out in the evening and know you're not flying till the next morning. If you're on standby, you can't guarantee you won't get called to fly in the middle of the night."

Chance nodded. It made sense. "You care about the people who work for you, don't you?"

She shrugged. "I see it as just basic human decency, but yes, I do care. They're my team, I'm closer to them than I am to anyone else. It's like you with the horses. Randy and Ron and the others, we work together, they're my buddies."

Chance smiled as the golf cart came to a halt outside the building and he spotted Missy waving at them through the window. "Are you ready for this?" he asked Hope.

She nodded nervously. He loved that about her. She was supposed to be this big name, this celebrity of sorts who the press hounded, but she was just a straightforward girl who got nervous about meeting new people, or at least about meeting people who were important to him. He took hold of her hand, wanting to show her he had her back. She looked up into his eyes and smiled, making him laugh. "For God's sake, please don't say I'm sweet."

She laughed and shook her head. "I wasn't about to; I was about to thank you for doing that." She looked down at their joined hands. "I don't feel nervous any more. You made me feel safe."

He didn't have time to answer before the automatic door slid open and Missy hurried to greet them. She threw herself at him and hugged him. "Chancey! I'm so glad you made it."

He laughed. "I know you don't like to fly, Miss, but we were hardly likely to fall out of the sky on the way here."

She made a face at him. "You know I didn't mean that. I just meant I've been waiting so long for you to come." She turned to Hope. "And to meet you."

Hope offered her hand, but Missy waved it away and reached up to hug her. "You'll get used to me, hon. I don't do formal." Chance was glad to see Hope smile as she hugged Missy back. "Good to know. I've been trying to get away from it myself."

Missy stood back with a grin. "Then you stick with me. I'll teach you."

Dan stepped forward with a shy smile. "It's a pleasure to meet you. I'm Dan." Chance knew he wasn't much of a hugger, but he stepped forward and briefly embraced Hope. Chance was proud of him. He'd overcome his own discomfort at the thought of having to hug a stranger because Hope had said she was trying to get away from being formal.

"It's a pleasure to meet you, too. I've heard so much about you."

Dan raised an eyebrow at Chance.

He winked. "What can I say? I like to brag about you. Not many guys can claim to have a multi-millionaire genius for a brother-in-law now, can they?" He felt bad when he'd said it. Dan looked embarrassed.

Hope smiled at him. "I'll admit I was a little awestruck when I realized who you were. Prometheus was huge when you started it."

Dan looked surprised that she knew him. Prometheus was the tech company he'd founded while he was still in college and had sold for millions when he moved here to the lake. He nodded. "We did well."

"It didn't do too well without you though, did it?"

He shook his head. "They sold out to Systech. Technically the company was no longer Prometheus the second I walked out the door. I kept the name."

"Yeah, but they still tried to use its reputation—your reputation—for far too long afterward," said Missy with a scowl.

Dan smiled at Hope and shrugged. "It's all history now. It doesn't matter. Your cousin took down Systech at the beginning of the year."

"Do you know him?"

"A little. We've met a few times, and it's always an interesting conversation when we do."

"I'll bet. We should get the two of you together."

"I'd like that." Chance was surprised how pleased Dan looked at that prospect, but he shouldn't be. He imagined Dan would love any chance he got to talk to another mind like his. Most of the time he was surrounded by mere mortals.

Missy smiled. "You'll be my hero if you can get him together with someone he can have a decent conversation with. My mundane chatter drives him nuts."

Chance tried not to laugh at the look on Dan's face. "But I love you," he said.

Missy wrinkled her nose at him and slipped her arm through his. "You must do to put up with me. Come on. We should get the bags taken care of and get these two home. Scot's waiting."

~ ~ ~

Hope looked around as Dan drove them into town. It was beautiful here. The mountains seemed to huddle around the lake protectively. As they got into the town itself she was surprised how busy it was. There were people out walking down Main Street and a thriving little shopping district. She felt like they'd been transported back in time, back to a simpler, happier time.

"Welcome to Summer Lake," said Missy as they drove by a large square that fronted onto the lake. "That's the resort and see that place on the water's edge? That's the Boathouse, where," she turned around to look at Chance, "I hope you'll come and join everyone for dinner tomorrow night."

She felt Chance tense beside her and saw him narrow his eyes at Missy. Missy shrugged. "I only said I hope. I'm not trying to force you or anything. But it'd be nice if you want to. That's all."

Chance nodded, but didn't speak.

"Thanks, Missy. I'd like to see the place. Even if we don't feel up to going out tomorrow night, perhaps you and I can stop in for lunch or something?"

Chance took hold of her hand and squeezed it.

Missy's grin spread across her face. "Sorry. I'm not known for being subtle. I say it like I see it, but damn, girl, you're good for him. You've got him figured out, haven't you?"

Hope chuckled, glad that Missy understood that she was simply looking out for Chance, not being stand-offish about meeting all their friends. "I think so. The fact that I'm even here is a big deal," she looked at Chance, "for both of us. We have to take everything slowly and if something doesn't feel comfortable we don't have to do it. Hopefully this is just my first visit of many."

Missy nodded and grinned at Chance. "She's a keeper, you'd better not screw it up."

Chance rolled his eyes at her. "I don't plan to, but my little sister might screw it up for me."

Missy stuck her tongue out at him and turned back to Hope. "I don't know how you put up with him. He can be moody, broody, and mean. I think you and I should go out for lunch or something just to get away from him for a while."

Hope laughed. "We probably should." She squeezed his hand again as she said, "I'm sure he'll need some time to himself anyway."

Dan continued driving down Main Street. The traffic thinned out the farther they went and soon they were in more of a leafy, broad avenue. The houses were larger out here and they backed onto the lake. A few minutes later, Dan pulled into the driveway of a beautiful big house and brought the Jeep to a halt outside.

"Come on in," said Missy. "I told Dad we'd call them when you arrived, but I wanted you to meet Scotty before we go over there."

"This is a beautiful home," said Hope once they were inside.

"Thanks," said Missy. "I absolutely love this place. Can you believe it was my favorite house in the world when I was growing up, and now, thanks to this guy," she put her hands on Dan's shoulders and reached up to peck his lips, "I get to live here. I never thought I would. When I was a kid, my friend used to come over from England to visit her grandparents who owned this place." She smiled. "She lives here, too, now, but that's another story."

Chance shook his head at her. "It is. We want to see Scotty, not listen to you tell Charlie's story."

Missy made a face at him and went to the bottom of the stairs. "Scot? We're back. Uncle Chance is here and Hope." She looked back at them with a smile. "For the longest time, he seemed like he was so much younger than his age. I thought maybe I'd ruined him and made him into a momma's boy, but he's caught up lately. He's gone all teenager on us. He's probably got his earphones in and can't even hear me."

"I'll go get him." Chance looked at Hope; he was checking that she was okay to be left alone.

She smirked at him and knew that he understood—it was so sweet of him to check, but she was fine. He narrowed his eyes at her, then bounded up the stairs. "Hey, Scotty! Where are you, bud?"

"Come on through to the kitchen," said Missy. "They'll probably be a minute. They're the most unlikely pair, but Scot loves his Uncle Chance."

"How hard is it?" asked Missy once they were seated at the island in the kitchen.

Hope raised an eyebrow. She thought she understood what Missy meant, but she didn't want to answer a question that wasn't being asked.

Missy wrinkled her nose seeming to wonder how to phrase it. "Tell me to butt out, if you like. I won't be offended, but like I told you, I tend to be pretty upfront about everything. I'm so happy you two have found each other, and you sure seem to understand each other, but it can't be easy. I thought he'd never let a woman into his life. Hell, he barely lets anyone in, and he doesn't let anyone get close. I'm just worried that he might give you a hard time—without meaning to—while he

figures out how to cope with being with someone. Someone who ..."
Hope smiled. "Someone who isn't Chloe."
Missy nodded. "Yeah. That."
"It's okay. You can say whatever you like to me. I tend to be quite straightforward myself, and I don't take offense easily, so you've got no worries there. We haven't had the easiest ride. It's difficult for him, but we're lucky that we're both willing to talk about it. We're honest with each other and we don't hide anything. Even if it hurts."
Missy nodded. "Wow. To get him talking at all is a big achievement, but to get him to be honest about what he feels is a miracle."
Hope smiled. "It didn't just happen with the wave of a wand; we've had to work just to get to where we are right now, but again, we've both been willing to." She met Missy's gaze. "I'm no stranger to grief myself and I think that helps. I won't claim to understand how he feels. Every loss is as unique as the person and the relationship that's gone, but I do understand that he needs to feel whatever he does, and I don't take it personally."
Missy gave her a puzzled look.
"I mean, knowing that he still loves Chloe, that he always will, doesn't make me feel that he doesn't love me. I don't feel like I'm second place, just in a different place."
"Wow." Missy shook her head. "You're perfect for him. I never thought he'd be able to leave Chloe in the past and step into a future with someone else."
Hope shook her head rapidly. "And you're right. He can't leave her behind. He doesn't need to and he shouldn't have to. She's a part of him, she helped make him who he is, she goes with him in his heart. This probably sounds too weird, but I feel like I love Chloe too. She's a part of him, you know?"

"Oh, hon!" Missy slid down from her stool and came to give Hope a hug. "You are awesome. I don't know many women who wouldn't feel threatened somehow by her memory. But you, the way you look at it, you're right, it's a much better way to look at things. He was tied to the past, and you've set him free by telling him he can take her with him. Damn, how did you get so smart?"

Hope gave her a sad smile. "I told you, I'm no stranger to grief myself. My mom died when I was twelve, and my dad reacted in the very same way Chance did. He moved us away from our home, he shut everyone out who reminded him of her."

"Including you?"

"Yeah. He didn't mean to hurt me, he just couldn't see past his own pain."

"Oh, I'm so sorry, honey."

Hope shrugged. "It is what it is. I learned to cope, and one of the ways I did that was by choosing to believe that my mom was still with me. I knew she was gone from this world, but I decided that I would carry her with me in my heart, then she'd never really be gone."

Missy's eyes filled with tears. "And you were just twelve?"

"Yeah, but that was a long time ago. And she's still in here." Hope tapped her heart. "And thanks to Chance, I'm rebuilding my relationship with my dad and he's starting to heal finally, too."

"Thanks to Chance?"

Hope smiled. "My dad came back to see him off. He thought Chance was going to be no-good, but when he met him, I think he saw a mirror image of himself. I wouldn't go as far as to say they've become friends—not yet, anyway, but they do like and respect each other."

Missy grinned. "That's awesome! I hate to say it, but your dad doesn't come across as an easy man."

"He isn't, but then neither is Chance. Sometimes the toughest nuts to crack are the sweetest."

Missy laughed and looked past Hope to where Chance was coming into the kitchen. He narrowed his eyes at her. "If she starts telling you I'm sweet, don't buy a word of it, Miss. You know me better than that."

Hope laughed. "That's not what I was saying at all."

"Good. Anyway, look who I disconnected from his computer." He stepped aside and a teenage boy smiled shyly at her.

"Hi."

"Hi, Scot. It's nice to meet you."

He nodded and then looked down at his feet.

"Are you going to come over to Poppy Jim's with us later?" asked Missy.

Scot looked up at her from under his eyebrows. "Do I have to?"

"No," said Chance. He spoke to Scot, but looked at Missy. "You shouldn't have to come and sit and listen to a bunch of old folks gas-bagging. I don't want you to start dreading me coming to town."

Scot smiled at him. "I'll never do that, Uncle Chance. I look forward to it."

"He does." Missy smiled at Hope. "You wouldn't think the computer guy and the cowboy would get along so well, but they always have."

"Hey," said Chance with a smile, "we make a good team. He's the brains, I'm the brawn."

Scot shook his head. "You're way smarter than I am."

Chance chuckled. "Don't kid yourself, shorty."

"There are different kinds of smart." Dan spoke up from his perch at the kitchen table. He'd been so quiet, Hope had forgotten he was there.

Missy went to him and patted his shoulder. "You know what that means, don't you, Chancey? It means we are well and truly outsmarted and they're both just too nice to say so."

"Oh, I know it, lil sis."

Scot looked up at them and smiled. "You must both be dumb to not understand what we mean. It's true, Mom. You're smart about all kinds of things that just blow my mind. And you, Uncle Chance, you're the same. Even though you're smart about different things than Mom is." He met Hope's gaze for a moment, then looked away again quickly before looking back. "I bet you're a different kind of smart, too. You must be."

"And why's that?" asked Missy.

"Because she has a big business, and because her dad is who he is, but most of all because she's with Uncle Chance." His cheeks were tinged with pink, but he met Hope's gaze and smiled. "That's a really smart move."

Hope smiled back, pleased that despite being so shy or just being an awkward teenager, she wasn't sure which it was, but either way, he'd made the effort to speak to her—and to tell her that she was smart to pick his Uncle Chance. "Thank you. I think so. In fact, I think it's the smartest move I've ever made."

Scot nodded, but his gaze had dropped to the floor again.

Missy smiled at her. "You must be smart to get him talking so much. This is the most he's said all week."

Scot looked up and rolled his eyes at her. "Yeah, and I think I just hit my word quota for the day. Can I go back to my room now?"

Missy scowled at him, but Chance spoke before she could. "Sure, bud. You get back to it. We'll catch up over the weekend, right?"

"Right." Scot smiled at him and gave Hope the slightest hint of a nod before heading back upstairs.

Chapter Six

Missy pulled up in front of their dad's house and turned in her seat to look back at Chance. "We're not going to stay too long. Dad's so excited you're both here and I just want to see how happy he is when he sees you. We'll make our excuses after about ten minutes and leave you to it."

"You don't have to," said Chance. He'd been thinking that this visit would be a kind of family reunion.

"I know, but I figured you'd want them to yourselves for a while. And I've invited them to come over for lunch on Sunday. Dan's smoking prime rib and I'm doing all the trimmings, in the hope that'll be enough to make you come over before you have to leave."

Chance smiled. She knew prime rib was his favorite. He looked at Hope and she nodded. "That'd be awesome, thanks, Miss."

She grinned. "It's a small price to pay to have all my family in my home for once."

Chance knew how much that meant to her. She hadn't had it easy in life. She'd had Scot when she was just a teenager and had raised him by herself until she met Dan a few years ago. The rift between Chance and his dad had been hard on her. He knew that their newfound closeness meant the world to her, and she would do anything she could to nurture it and draw their family back together.

They all turned at the sound of a shout from the house. Chance chuckled when he saw his dad standing in the open doorway, leaning on the frame and waving his cane at them. "If you're going to sit out there all afternoon, would you at least send Hope in? I'm not worried about the rest of you. Well, send Dan, too."

They all laughed and got out of the car. "Sorry, Dad," called Chance. "It's Missy. You know what she's like. She started talking and wouldn't shut up long enough for us to get out." He came around the car and joined Hope, not wanting to leave her behind as he went to greet his dad. He needn't have worried, she hurried by him and went straight to his dad and hugged him.

"Hey, Frank. It's good to see you. You're looking a lot fitter than you were in Oregon."

"That's all thanks to your uncle." He grinned and hugged her tightly with one arm, supporting himself against the door with the other. Chance understood a little about where his pride came from in that moment. His dad could have leaned on Hope to hug her, but he wouldn't let her support his weight. He'd rather cling to the door frame and support himself—even though it meant he got less of a hug because of it. He pursed his lips and tucked that thought away for further examination later.

"Would you let go of her and give me a turn?" Alice appeared in the doorway and Chance was grateful to her, as he was so often. She'd spotted that his dad was struggling now to keep himself upright. She pretended to push him away, but what she was really doing was setting him straight again with his weight balanced properly and his cane for support. Chance caught her eye as she hugged Hope and gave her a nod, hoping that she understood he'd noticed and he loved her for it. He picked up where she'd left off and put his arm around his dad's shoulders, hustling him back inside the house and back to his place on the sofa. "How come I never get a hug like that; huh, Pops?"

Chance sat down next to him and leaned in for a hug. His eyes filled with tears as his dad hugged him back. He'd always been a wiry kind of guy, but in that hug Chance could feel how much skinnier he was, and how little strength he had. He had to bury his face in his dad's shoulder and blink away the tears before he dared let anyone see him. When he came back up, Hope caught his eye. She'd seen. She understood. She gave him a sad smile. He hated to think that it wouldn't be too many years before his dad was gone.

"What about me?" asked Missy with a grin. "Do I get forgotten, now the prodigal son's back?"

Chance knew she was joking, but for a moment, his dad looked stricken. "You'll never be forgotten, love. Come here." He held his arm out to her and the three of them shared a hug that had Chance's eyes filling up again.

After a few moments Alice asked Hope if she wanted to help her in the kitchen, and, of course, his dad looked up at that. "She's not the help, Alice! She's a guest. A very special guest." He winked at Hope. "And a fancy one, too. You can't be asking her to help in the kitchen."

Hope laughed. "I'd like to."

Alice winked at her. "There's no need, sweetie. Everything's ready and I'm going to ask my Danny to carry it through for us. I just knew that as soon as I said that, Frank would stop strangling those two and come up for air."

"She spoils all my fun, that one." His dad pretended to glare at Alice, but Chance could see the love that shone in his eyes. It seemed that opening his own heart up to love was allowing him to see the love all around him. His dad and Alice, Missy and Dan; they had great relationships and so much love. He wanted to believe that he and Hope would grow to share something like that.

Dan brought the tray through from the kitchen, and once Alice had given everyone a drink, they all sat there staring at each other for a minute until Missy laughed. "Well, this is awkward silence. It's not like us, is it?" She looked at Hope.

"You must have him in awe. I thought he'd be chattering away; he's been chattering about you for weeks."

"I'm just having a sip of my tea, thank you, Melissa. Then," he turned and looked Chance in the eye, "I'm going to start asking questions, like when are you going to make an honest woman of her?"

"Dad!" Missy shot Chance a worried look, but he smiled reassuringly. "Don't worry, Miss. It's not the first time he's asked, is it, Hope?"

"No," she answered with a smile.

"It'll be the first time I get an answer though," his dad persisted. "So, when are you thinking? I'm guessing it's going to be up there in Montana, right?" He nodded at Hope. "You'll want to have your wedding where your people are?"

Hope nodded hesitantly, then looked at Chance. "We haven't talked about it yet."

"See, Dad." Missy scowled at him. "You leave them alone and let them tell you in their own time."

He scowled at her, but he did look a little remorseful. "Okay, okay. I'm just impatient." He looked at Hope. "Forgive me? I didn't mean to …" He shrugged and took another sip of his tea looking disgruntled.

"There's nothing to forgive, Frank," Hope reassured him. "I wish I could answer you, and I will, just as soon as I know."

His dad glowered at Chance. "See, she's waiting on you. You'd better get your act together, son, or she might get tired of waiting."

Chance smiled. "You're right. I should, and when I do, you'll be the first to know."

"There," said Alice firmly. "You heard that, Frank? You'll be the first to know. So, until then, would you please stop harassing them about it?"

He shrugged and muttered to himself, then looked up and winked at Hope. "I can hope, right?"

She chuckled. "You can, and I think you have a very good chance."

Chance groaned. "Don't get her started on playing with our names."

Missy laughed. "It's hard not to, isn't it? I mean there are so many possibilities. You've found Hope. She has a Chance."

"Yeah, yeah, all right." Chance waved his hand at her. "We've heard them all."

Hope smiled at her. "To be fair, he's usually the one who comes up with them."

Missy laughed. "But he says it's corny when we do it? That sounds about right."

Chance nodded. He noticed that his dad was looking worried and rubbing his knuckles, which he always did when something was troubling him. "What's up, Dad?"

He frowned. "I'm not sure I should say."

"Try it, and see."

He rubbed his knuckles some more, then met Chance's gaze. "I'm not trying to rush the two of you along, I just want to know when it'll be. I need to figure out how I'm going to get there." Chance felt terrible when he saw the worry in his dad's eyes. "I made it to our Miss and Dan's wedding, but only just. I never thought I'd see the day you'd tie the knot, not since … But now, I know you will." He smiled at Hope. "You've found her and I want more than anything in the world to watch the two of you get wed before I die."

"And you will."

He blew out a big sigh. "Son, I put on a good front and Alice covers for me, bless her heart, but I'm not up to doing much more traveling. Montana's a long way. It takes you a couple of days to drive here. I don't know how I'm going to manage a trip like that, but I'm going to do it somehow."

Chance's heart ached for him. His dad was a proud man and he'd been a strong, fit man all his life until the stroke. Chance hated to see him so worried about something that would have been so minor to him not so long ago.

Hope squeezed Chance's hand and raised an eyebrow. He knew what she wanted to say, and loved her for checking with him before she spoke. He nodded.

"Frank, if it is in Montana, and we haven't decided yet, but if it is, you don't need to go by car. You don't need to go by car wherever it is."

He looked at her. "What do you mean?"

"We can send the plane for you."

His brows knit together. "But the plane belongs to Dan's brother, Jack. He let him use it for me when I had to get to Miss's wedding.

"And he'd let you use it again, anytime you want to," said Dan. "But I don't like to ask. It's not right. He's been kind and he's almost family, but …"

"You don't need to ask him," said Hope. "We have a plane, too. We can send it to get you when we get married. Whenever you want to go anywhere, we can send it for you."

His dad looked at Chance. "You have a plane now?"

Chance hesitated. He couldn't say yes, but he didn't want to point out that it was Hope's plane.

She answered for him. "We do." She squeezed his hand again and he nodded.

His dad smiled. "That's nifty, huh?"

"It is. I'm lucky. It's not like I earned it, not like Dan or his brother." She smiled at Dan, and once again Chance loved the way she tried to keep everyone happy. She didn't want to ruffle any feathers, but she'd learn with time that's Dan's feathers didn't ruffle easily.

Dan smiled back at her. He knew what she was doing. He didn't need appeasing, but he no doubt appreciated her effort.

"When we get married …"

"So, it's definitely a when, not an if?" asked his dad.

Chance laughed. "You don't miss a trick, do you?"

"Nope. And we can leave it alone now, if you want. I've heard all I need to. You are getting married and I don't have to worry how to get there."

Hope smiled at him. "Good, I'm glad we could set your mind at ease."

"Nearly," his smile faded again. "Just promise me you won't take too long about it? I want to still be around to see it."

"Don't, Dad." Missy voice sounded a little too high, and Chance knew that the thought of him dying was upsetting her. "You might have heard all you need to, but I still have a question."

"What's that?" asked Chance.

"Have you even asked her yet?" She gave Hope an apologetic smile. "Sorry, hon, but I don't see a ring, and all this talking about it before you've even asked just seems wrong to me."
Hope smiled. "It's okay."
The way she said it told Chance that maybe it wasn't as okay as he'd thought. He glowered at Missy, but he didn't know what to say, because it seemed she had a point.
She shrugged and he was grateful she didn't say any more, but she'd said enough to make him realize that it was time to put some serious thought into his proposal—and when they got back to the valley, it'd be time to go see Seymour and officially ask for his blessing.

~ ~ ~

When they left Frank and Alice's place, Missy drove them over to the resort where they'd booked a room for the next couple of nights. She'd said she and Dan would leave after a short time, but Frank had asked them to stay and Hope was glad of it. Chance had told her most of his family history and she knew that the three of them didn't get to spend much time together. She wanted them to cherish every moment they got. Plus, she enjoyed Missy's company—and Dan's too, even though he didn't say much. Chance had been right, it was worth listening whenever he did speak. She was planning to call Oscar whenever she got a minute. She'd love to get him together with Dan; she just knew they'd enjoy each other's company.
Missy drove through the resort and pulled up outside a beautiful cabin that sat by itself, right on its own little beach.
"This place is amazing!" said Hope.

Missy turned to smile at her. "I'm glad you like it. It's not one of those fancy five-star resorts, but it's a great place, and the guy who owns it is one of my best friends."

"How is Ben?" asked Chance.

Missy grinned. "Ben is finally happy! You have no idea how good it feels to be able to say that."

Chance grinned back at her. "I think I do have some idea. It took him half his life to get there, but if anyone deserves to be happy, it's Ben."

Hope wondered if he was comparing himself to this Ben. It'd taken Chance half his life to even consider the possibility of being happy.

Missy smiled at her. "Sorry to talk about people you don't know yet, but you'll meet him before the weekend's over I'm sure. Even if you don't come out tomorrow night, you'll see him around the resort. He's a very hands-on owner."

Chance chuckled. "And how's Charlie doing? Does she ever get to see him, or does he still spend all his time here?"

"You'd be surprised how much less he works these days."

"She put her foot down then?" asked Chance.

Missy shook her head with a big grin. "Nope. He cut back his hours voluntarily, as soon as they got married. He's so cute. He wants to spend as much time as he can with her. In fact, when I saw her the other day she told me that he's been asking her to cut her work schedule back."

Chance laughed. "Who would ever have believed that?"

Dan smiled at Hope. "Ben's family has owned the resort forever. He's run the place since he was a teenager. To call him a workaholic would be an understatement. He and Charlie were together when they were teens, but they broke up and she went back to England. They never got over each other and she came back just last year. They're married now."

Missy nodded. "Remember I told you I had a friend who came over from England every summer when we were kids? Well, that was Charlotte."

Hope smiled. "I envy you, having friends around who you grew up with."

Missy laughed. "Oh, you have no idea. You'll meet most of them tomorrow night, but there are a couple dozen of us who all grew up here and have now moved back and are settling down and having families." She looked at Chance. "I don't suppose there's any way you'd ever consider coming back?"

Hope looked at him. She thought she knew what he'd say, but he surprised her. "I don't think so, but I'd never say never." Wow! Hope had thought that'd be exactly what he'd say. He smiled at her. "If you like the idea of living in a small town with a great bunch of friends, then maybe this is where you'd want to be?"

She didn't know what to say. She thought they already had that in Montana, and she was surprised Chance would even consider living here. This was Chloe's town.

Missy gave her an apologetic look. "Sorry, hon. It's not like you have to decide now or anything, I was just curious."

"I'd never say never, either," she said with a smile. "But to be honest, I've only just got back to Montana. To me, that's going back to my hometown. I don't have any old friends there, but through Chance, I've met a whole bunch of new ones. Plus, my dad's come back, too." She looked at Chance. "Maybe someday?"

He nodded, but she wasn't sure what he was thinking.

"You're doing it again, Miss," said Dan.

"Doing what?"

He smiled. "Making everyone sit outside in the car talking, when we should be getting going."

"Oh. Sorry." She got out and the rest of them followed her.

"I got you all booked in and sorted out, so you don't have to go up to the lodge if you don't want to. Here's the key and the little information package." She handed them over to Hope.

"Thanks. Don't you want to come in?"

Missy smiled. "I'd love to, but I've hogged too much of your time already, and I told Scotty we wouldn't be gone too long when we went to Dad's." She rummaged in her purse and pulled out another key and an envelope, then turned and pointed at the car sitting outside the cabin. "I got you a rental car. You might not need it, but I didn't want you to feel stuck if you want to explore or anything."

Chance took the key with a smile. "Thanks, Miss. I didn't know anyone did car rentals."

"They do now. One of Smoke's student pilots used to work for one of the big franchises and he's set up his own branch out at the airport. He seems to be doing good business, too."

Chance nodded. "That's good to know, and thanks for setting it up. I'll pay you back when …"

"Oh, shush! You'll do no such thing."

Hope had to laugh at the expression on Chance's face. She had a feeling Missy was the only person in the world who'd get away with telling him to shush.

Even Missy seemed to know that she'd pushed her luck. "You can take care of our rental when we come up there to visit you, how about that?"

Chance nodded. "Okay, you've got yourself a deal."

Dan smiled at them. "Sorry guys. I got us out of the car, but she's still not letting you go, so I'll just have to drag her away."

"Okay, okay." She smiled at Hope. "I really will let you go now. I'm leaving it up to you, how much you want to see of us, but we'll be around all weekend if you want to call or just drop in."

Dan chuckled and looked at Chance. "She won't beg you, but I will. Please, at least call, or I'll have to listen to her fretting the whole time."

"Don't worry. I'll keep you posted on what we're up to and when we will be seeing you. You're a big part of why we're here."

Missy reached up and hugged him. "Aww, that makes me so happy." She turned to hug Hope, too.

Chance shook his head at her. "I'm glad, but will you go now?"

Missy laughed and got back in the car. "Okay. I'm going."

Chapter Seven

When Missy and Dan had gone, Chance unlocked the door of the cabin and let Hope go in ahead of him. "I know it's not up to the same standards you're used to, but the resort is the best the area has to offer and …"

"Oh, shush!" said Hope. He narrowed his eyes at her and she laughed. "You can't say anything. Missy gets away with telling you to shush."

He rolled his eyes. "I knew getting the two of you together was a bad idea."

She came to him with a smile and slid her arms around his waist. "You don't mean that. You love it really, don't you?"

He nodded. "I do, though I'm sure I'll live to regret it."

"You probably will, but not today. Maybe after we have lunch together tomorrow."

"You're going to do that?"

"I'd like to. You know what girls are like; we like to get the menfolk out of the way before we can really talk." He raised an eyebrow. He didn't think of her as a girly girl or a gossipy one. She smiled. "You know I'm only playing with you. I'd like to get to know her better, but my real reason for suggesting it is to give you some time by yourself. I'm sure there are things you want to do. Places you want to go." She shrugged. "I'm sure you'll need some time alone in your head."

He nodded, grateful that she understood him so well and didn't want to try to change him—or to be with him every minute of the day. Until he'd met the girls who were now Remingtons, he'd believed that most women were clingy and needy. He knew better now and was glad Hope was as independent as she was. "Well, if you want to have lunch with her, I'm sure I can entertain myself for a while."

She smiled. "You take as long as you need."

"Thanks, honey. So, that's tomorrow afternoon taken care of; what do you want to do with the rest of our time here?"

She shrugged. "My plan is simply to follow your lead. This is your place; we're here to see your family and your friends if you want to. Do you have any interest in going out with them all tomorrow night?"

Chance blew out a sigh. "Can we play that one by ear? I'd love to see them all, but seeing them all at once is a bit overwhelming. But then maybe it's better that way. If we get them all out of the way in one go, it'll be quicker than making time to stop and see different ones. What do you think?"

"I think we should play it by ear, like you say. I'm happy to go along with anything and you need to see how you feel at the time."

"Yeah." He knew he'd have to see how he felt. "So far, I'm doing okay. I like having you here. I like that my dad and Miss love you so much." He hesitated, not sure if he should continue.

"But we don't know how you'll feel as the weekend goes on. It might feel wrong for me to be here."

He nodded, glad she understood.

"It's okay. I was thinking the same thing. I'm sure it'll get harder as the memories hit you. Certain places, certain people will act as triggers."

"Yeah. I've said I'll see Gabe and Renée, and that's probably the one I'm most concerned about. I'm probably closer to them than the others; we were in the same grade. But I'll admit that I feel bad introducing you to Renée." He closed his arms tighter around her. "I know it's dumb. I know she'll love you, and she's told me over and over that she's happy for me. But she's Chloe's sister, you know?"

"I think I do know. I think it'll be tough for you. But I do want to ask you something."

"What?"

"If she's okay with it, would you ask if I could meet her?"

"I'll take you with me, if you want to go."

"I do want to go, but I think you and she would be more comfortable if I'm not there. At least not for all of it. I could meet you after a while, or if she's okay with it, I could meet her by myself later."

Chance nodded slowly. "Maybe that would be better." He dropped a kiss on the top of her head. "I don't know if I should say this, but I want to go to the cemetery." He felt himself tense as he waited for her reaction. He felt like he'd just told her he wanted to go cheat on her while they were here.

She didn't seem to see it that way, though. "I didn't think there'd be any question that you would."

"You don't mind?"

She looked up into his eyes. "Chance, you need to accept that I really don't mind. I understand." She sighed. "We all deal with grief in different ways, but I think wanting to go to the cemetery or wherever we feel close to our loved ones is pretty universal."

He nodded. "Thanks. You know, it's not like it was when we first met. Back in Oregon, I didn't think I could let myself feel for you, without detracting from Chloe somehow. Now I'm coming to see that maybe the way I've cared for Chloe; as if she were still here, is detracting from you somehow."

"But it's not; I don't mind."

"I know. Let me see if I can explain it better. It's not so much that it's taking anything away from you, as it's taking something away from us. I want to be all in with you. I want us to be a team, a real couple, like my dad and Alice and Missy and Dan. It can't be that way until I let go …"

"You don't have to let her go!"

"I do, honey; I get that now. She's already gone, she's been gone for nearly nineteen years. I'm not holding her here, I'm just holding on. But what I've been holding onto is the pain. That's what I need to let go of—the pain and the anger."

She nodded slowly.

"Does that make sense?"

"It does. It makes all the sense in the world."

"Yeah. I just wish I'd figured it out sooner."

"You've figured it out now; that's all that matters."

He smiled. "I love that you always try to find the bright side."

"I'm hoping I'll be able to teach you to do the same."

"Me too."

~ ~ ~

A little while later, they sat out on the deck in front of the cabin. "It's just so beautiful here." Hope realized that must be the fifth time she'd said it.

Chance smiled. "You mean it, don't you?"

She laughed. "I really do. I wouldn't keep repeating myself if I didn't."

"I'm glad. It's a great place, and I feel a kind of loyalty to it. I wanted you to love it, but I didn't think it'd be grand enough for you. It's just a small town, and the resort isn't …"

"Would you please stop that? I love small towns, I grew up in one, remember? This place just feels good. And okay, so maybe the resort isn't the Ritz, but it's well-kept and from what I've seen so far, it's well run. I don't need, and if I'm honest, I don't really enjoy the fancy places. They rarely feel good; more often than not they're snooty."

"They are, but you're not."

"I hope not."

"You're not. Not one bit. I should get over worrying about whether things are good enough for you, shouldn't I?"

She smiled. "I wish you would. I'll let you know if I don't like something."

"Good, then I can relax."

"Speaking of which, do you think we've done enough relaxing? I mean, I love sitting here, the view is amazing, but I'd like to get out and do something, if you want to?"

"I'd love to. What do you want to do?"

"Anything. We could go for a walk. We could go up to the lodge and see if your friend is around if you want to see him. Or whatever you think. You know what there is to do and who you want to see."

Chance pressed his lips together and she waited, wondering if she was pushing him too hard or if he'd rather just hangout and hideout here. "We could go up and see if Ben's around?"

She nodded. "Let's do that. It'll be fun to explore the resort, too. I love what I've seen so far."

Chance got up and offered her his hand. On the way out, he grabbed his baseball cap from the table in the hallway.

"I wondered if you'd wear your cowboy hat and boots here."

"I do most of the time, because I feel kind of naked without them, but since I picked this thing up," he tugged the peak of his cap, "I feel better. I've still got something on my head and I don't get the odd looks."

She laughed. "Odd looks? I think you look sexy in your hat."

He shook his head at her. "Apparently a lot of guys wear them for just that reason. Which is why I don't like to. I don't want to look like a poser."
She laughed. "But you're not, you're the genuine article, the real McCoy."
"I am a genuine cowboy, yeah, but I don't want to be stopped and get into a conversation about it, so the cap's good. You don't like it?"
"I do. I think that's sexy, too."
"You think everything's sexy."
"I do, everything about you, that is."
He shook his head at her. "You're a sweet talker. Maybe we shouldn't stay out too long. I'll show you something sexy when we get back."
"Ooh, yes, please!"
He chuckled and led her out of the cabin. "Come on, let's go before I change my mind and show you right now."
As they walked up the path between the cabins, Hope looked around taking everything in. She sniffed the air. "It even smells good here."
"Yeah, it's the mixture of pine and lake, I think. To me it's the smell of home."
She nodded, wondering if she'd made him remember too much. She knew smells were strongly associated with memory.
As they got closer to the center of the resort, Chance pointed at the big two-story building with decks out over the lake. "That's the Boathouse. It's like the hub of all social life around here. People meet up for breakfast, the girls meet up for lunch on Saturdays. There's live music on the weekends; the house band is really good and they're good guys, too."
"It sounds wonderful."
"It is, it's a good place."

"Has it always been here?" What she really wanted to know was how many memories it might hold for him.

"It has, but not like it is now. When I was a kid it was more of a bar with a bit that served some food. Ben added the decks a few years back, and he brought in the band and started serving breakfast. He's done a lot to turn the place around."

"He's done a good job of it."

Chance smiled and pointed at a guy who was coming down the steps from the main lodge. "You can tell him that, there he is."

Ben looked at them and smiled. "Chance! Damn, it's good to see you." He smiled at Hope. "And I can't tell you how happy I am to meet you." He held his hand out. "Ben Walton. I'm an old friend."

Hope smiled as she shook with him. "It's lovely to meet you, Ben."

Chance nodded. "I don't know how much time we'll get this weekend, but you need to get to know Ben and Charlie."

"We'd love to hang out with you. In fact, let me know when you've got some free time and we'll come up there to visit," said Ben.

Chance laughed. "Miss wasn't lying when she told me your workaholic days are over then?"

Ben laughed with him. "No, she wasn't." He looked at Hope, wanting to include her. "I've dedicated my whole life to running this place. People have always given me a hard time about how much I worked, but I got married last year and my priorities have changed."

Hope smiled. She already liked Ben immensely; he was just one of those people who put you at ease and made you feel like an old friend. "I'll bet your wife's happy about that."

"She is. She wanted me to ease back a bit and I have, now it's me asking her to take more time off."

"What's she doing?" asked Chance.

"She set herself up a marketing company. She manages social media and online marketing for pretty much everyone in town, or at least it seems that way. She does work for Holly and Laura for their stores, and Lily for the riding stables. She even set up the main tourism site for the town, and, of course, she does all the marketing for the resort."

"Wow, she must be busy," said Hope.

Ben gave her a rueful smile. "Now you see where I'm coming from. I've finally slowed down, and she's working all the time. I can't complain. It's good to see her happy doing something she loves."

Hope nodded. She was hoping to find herself in that situation soon.

"I can't stop for long right now. Kenzie needs me to bring her some change in the bar. Do you want to come in for a drink?"

Chance pursed his lips. "Who's in there?"

"I left about half an hour ago, but it was quiet in there." He cocked his head to one side. "Let's see. No one who'd pounce on you, I don't think. Emma was in earlier with Jack's mom and the baby, but they left before I did. April and Eddie were here, but I saw them leaving just now. No. I don't think there's anyone who would want to hog your time." He smiled at Hope. "He's a popular guy around here."

She laughed. "It seems he's a popular guy wherever he goes."

"Yeah, he just wishes he wasn't," said Chance. "Just because there's no one in there now doesn't mean they won't come in once we're there."

"No, sorry. I can't guarantee that."

Chance blew out a sigh. "Okay, we'll risk it."

Hope punched his arm. "It's okay, you just need to give me a signal or something if you want to leave. I can come up with a reason I have to go and then you can blame me and not seem rude."

Ben laughed and looked at Chance. "She knows you well, then?"

"She does, and she loves me, despite my flaws." Hope wasn't sure whether she or Ben was more surprised to hear him say that. Chance shrugged, looking a little surprised himself. "And I love her even more for understanding me."

Ben grinned at them. "You have no idea how happy I am for the two of you."

"I think I do, I'm just as happy for you and Charlie." Chance turned to her. "This guy was about as much of a lost cause as I was. Charlotte left here when they were both eighteen, but he never gave up on her. It took them all this time, but they're finally back together now."

Ben nodded. "Everyone thought I was crazy not to give up on her and move on, but I couldn't. This guy," he nodded at Chance, "was the one who kept telling me not to give up." He grinned suddenly. "Do you know what he used to tell me?"

Hope shook her head.

"He told me over and over again, where there's life there's hope."

The little hairs on the back of her neck stood up, and she smiled at Chance, who nodded. "I just had no idea how true that would turn out to be."

Ben smiled. "Sorry, I really need to get this change to Kenzie or she's going to be pissed."

Chance laughed and explained to Hope as they followed him inside. "Kenzie is awesome. You'll love her. She works for Ben and manages the bar, but sometimes you'd think he works for her."

Ben looked back at her and nodded. "Either that or you'd think she's my mom the way she carries on."

They followed him across the square and into the bar of the Boathouse. Hope loved it. It was so welcoming. There was a great feel to the place. Ben ducked behind the bar when they reached it and opened the cash register to tip the change into the drawer.

A slender, blonde woman came out from the back and scowled at him. "Don't tell me you're trying to sneak it in there? What took you so ... Oh!" She grinned at Chance and came over to greet them. "Hi, Chance! It's good to see you. And you," she nodded at Hope, making her feel a little less welcome than she had been.

Chance scowled at her and Ben turned back to join them. "Now, Kenzie, I want you to play nice, okay? This is Hope. Hope is Chance's lady and the reason we get to see him, and more importantly, the reason that he's happy these days."

Kenzie's face softened as she smiled. "You're happy?" she asked Chance, who smirked and nodded. She turned to Hope. "In that case, it's a real pleasure to meet you, lady."

Hope grinned, thrilled at the sudden change in Kenzie's demeanor. "And you."

"Sorry if I was a bit off at first. I've never seen him bring a woman in here. I tend to be a bit protective of these guys."

Ben nodded vigorously. "Kenzie cares about us all—ferociously."

Kenzie laughed. "I'm not ferocious. I just like to look after my own; and since you're with him," she jerked her chin at Chance, "you are now officially one of my own. So, what can I get you? It's on me."

"I'd love an orange juice, please."

"Okay, and what about you, Chance?"

"I'll take one of those, too."

When she left them to get the drinks, Ben winked at Hope. "Don't mind her. She's got a heart of gold underneath the brash exterior."

Kenzie came back and raised an eyebrow at him. "Did I just hear you call me trashy?"

"No!" said Ben.

"Hell, no!" added Chance.

"What I said was brash; you can be a bit brash."

Kenzie shrugged. "Probably. Take me or leave me, I am what I am. You can call me trashy if you want as long as you still love me."

"You know I do, and Charlie does, we all do."

"Good, that's okay then. Excuse me." She left them to go and serve a couple who'd just come in and taken a seat at the other end of the bar.

Chance shook his head as he watched her go. "She's a piece of work, that one."

"I like her," said Hope. "She's real."

Chance laughed. "That's one way of putting it."

"Uh-oh. I told you I couldn't guarantee that no one would come in. I forgot Jack and Pete were getting back from Seattle this afternoon. Here they come."

Hope looked at Chance nervously. "It's okay," he said. "They're good guys. Jack's a relative newcomer; Pete's the most logical and unemotional of the bunch."

Hope watched the two men make their way through the bar. They were both good-looking guys; nothing like Chance, but in a clean-cut business kind of way. They were both tall and muscular—one of them dark almost Latin-looking and the other much fairer, blonde with blue eyes.

"Chance Malone!" said the fairer of the two. "It's good to see you. Miss said you might be here this weekend."

Chance smiled. "Typical Missy, she knew I was coming, but she didn't know if I'd show my face more like it."

The guy grinned. "I didn't like to say it that way." He smiled at Hope. "Hi, I'm Pete Hemming, and you, I already know, are the one and only Hope Davenport."

Hope smiled and shook hands with him. "It's nice meet you," she said, wondering as she did why his name sounded familiar.

The other guy stepped forward. "Pleased to meet you. I'm Jack Benson and I should probably warn you about my wife," he said with a chuckle.

Hope raised an eyebrow as Chance groaned and Ben and Pete laughed.

"Would it be better if you explained?" Jack asked him.

Chance shook his head. "No, you go ahead. I wouldn't know what to say."

Hope waited, wondering what was coming. Jack seemed to sense her tension. "It's okay, it's nothing horrible, it's just been a standing joke around here since they were all growing up together. My wife, Emma, has had a crush on Chance here for the last, what? Twenty years?"

"Ha, it's getting on for thirty now," said Pete with a grin. "Don't worry," he told Hope. "She's harmless and I'm sure you'll get along with her, but she does tend to go a bit gaga over this guy. She loves Jack more than life itself, but there's something about the cowboy hat that makes her knees go weak."

Chance chuckled and tugged the brim of his baseball cap. "I'm hoping she might not recognize me in this."

Hope smiled. "I can't wait to meet her, I'm sure we will get along, we have the same taste in broody cowboys."

Ben nodded at her. "I think you'll hit it off. They're only teasing. Emma and Missy have been best friends since they were eight. Emma had a thing for her best friend's big brother like a lot of girls do."

Hope smiled. She hoped that Emma wouldn't mind them all joking about her like this. Hope would be uncomfortable, if she knew people were talking about her this way.

"Anyway," said Pete, moving the conversation along, which Hope liked him for. "I don't know if you know this, but our moms were best friends."

"Oh! Now I know why your name sounded so familiar. I didn't know anything about you till I told my dad we were coming here. He told me about your mom and how they lost touch, but he gave me your name and your parents number. I wasn't sure if I should look them up."

Pete nodded. "I know it'd mean a lot to them if you get the time." He looked at Chance. "Or I'm sure there'll be other opportunities if your weekend is all booked up."

Chance nodded. His lips were pressed together and his eyes were narrowed, and Hope realized she'd forgotten to tell him about her conversation with her dad about how he knew Summer Lake. She turned to him. "You know how Dad and I have been talking more lately? He mentioned a while back that he knew Summer Lake and when I told him we were coming I remembered to ask him how he knew it."

Chance nodded. He didn't seem annoyed that she hadn't told him, but there was something going on behind those pale blue eyes. She didn't know what it was, but she didn't want to ask him. She'd wait until they were alone.

"Are you coming out tomorrow night?" asked Jack.

"Maybe," said Chance.

Jack smiled. "I hope so. I just want to warn Emma to behave herself if you are."

Chance smiled. "She's fine, I can tell you now, that for the last twenty years or so I've kind of looked forward to seeing her. She was about the only person who made me feel that I might just be lovable."

"Aww," Jack shook his head. "Can I tell her that? That'll make her day."

Chance laughed. "Yeah." He looked at Hope. "Emma is one of the sweetest people you'll ever meet."

"She sounds like it."

Pete's phone buzzed and he checked it quickly, then looked at Chance. "I know what you're like about crowds. That was Gabe. He'd said he might drop in to talk business, but he's on his way here with Renée to meet Michael and Megan."

"Okay." Hope expected Chance to down his orange juice and get out of there, so she was pleasantly surprised when he consulted her first. "Are you ready? Do you mind if we go? Or would you rather stay?"

She nodded. "Let's go."

Chapter Eight

The next morning, they sat out on the deck watching the sun rise over the water. Chance was surprised how well he'd slept. He'd thought he might toss and turn all night, thinking about Chloe, but he hadn't. He hadn't really thought about her much at all since they arrived. He was more concerned with making sure that Hope enjoyed herself, that she was okay. It seemed he'd been right when he said he needed to let go of the pain. He'd clung to it all these years, but now he had happiness and he wanted to cling to that instead.

Hope sipped her coffee and smiled over at him. "What are you thinking?"

"That I want to hold on to Hope."

"Aww, and I want to grab hold of my Chance with both hands and never let go."

He chuckled. "Do think after a couple of years we'll finally give up on all the word plays?"

"I hope not."

He rolled his eyes.

"Don't look so grumpy, Chancey bear." That made him laugh in spite of himself. "What do you want to do today?"

He met her gaze. "I want to go see Renée, and I want to go to the cemetery. What I don't want to do is leave you by yourself."

"I'm a big girl, and I'm looking forward to a bit of time to myself. I want to get to know this place on my own terms, not just see it through your eyes."

"Okay, how do you want to work it, then?"

She shrugged. "Do you want to go do your thing and call me when you're ready to meet back here or somewhere else?"

"I can do, but do you want to do something together first? It'll only take me a couple of hours, and I figured, if you're going to have lunch with Miss, then I'll go and see Renée about then."

"Okay. How would you feel about going for a ride?"

He smirked. "Any time."

She wagged her finger at him. "Not that kind of ride. I mean horseback riding. I was looking through the literature on the coffee table and there's a riding stables that's part of the resort."

Chance nodded. "That's Lily. She's another one I went to school with."

"Wow, they're not joking when they say everyone knows everyone in a small town, are they?"

"Nope, they're deadly serious. You can see why I couldn't stay."

She nodded but didn't say anything.

"Did I say something wrong?"

"No, I was just thinking how idyllic life in a town like this must be, but it isn't really, is it? I was thinking that it'd be nice to live in a place where the press doesn't ever come. But even though there aren't reporters around every corner, everyone still gets to know your story and the details of your life."

"Yeah. The small-town grapevine might not reach as many people as the newspapers do, but it's maybe even more intrusive, because the people it does reach are the ones you run into every day."

Hope smiled brightly. "It doesn't matter though, does it? We don't live here, we're just visiting."

"We are." He smiled back. "And there's no press here and the people who know our business are all happy for us. So, come on, let's take a walk up to the barn and see if Lily's around. She might be busy with it being Saturday morning, but maybe she'll have a couple of horses to spare and let us take them out."

~ ~ ~

Hope smiled as they walked up the leafy lane that led to the riding stables. "I love this place."

"Me too. Lily's got a great setup here. I think you'll like her." He pursed his lips. "In fact, I think the two of you might find you have a lot in common. She comes from money. Not as much as you, but her family is very well-off. They lived here through her high school years, but then they moved back to Southern California somewhere. Malibu, I think. She went with them and tried to fit in to that world, but she hated it. She decided she'd rather do what she loved in a place she loves, so she came back here and set up the stables."

Hope smiled. "Now I really can't wait to meet her."

When they reached the big barn, Hope looked around, taking everything in. The place was well cared for and busy. It had the air of a successful happy place, and she had a feeling that was the result of Lily being successful and happy in what she was doing.

"Chance!" They both turned to see a petite, dark-haired woman standing in the doorway of a camper parked off to one side under the trees.

Chance grinned and went to greet her. "Hey, Lil. How's it going?"

"It's going great, Chance. Things couldn't be better." She smiled at Hope. "I'm sorry, but I've been so excited to meet you."

Hope smiled back. "Don't be sorry. I feel the same way about you. Chance told me how you left the SoCal life to come back here and do what you love. I'm impressed. I'm trying to make the same kind of move myself."

Lily's eyes lit up. "You're going to move to Montana?"

"I already have."

Lily hugged herself and did a little dance. "Oh, that's awesome, guys! I'm so happy for you."

Chance chuckled and nodded. "Thanks, Lil."

She nodded, looking at little embarrassed. "Sorry, you'll have to forgive my enthusiasm. It's just I, well, we all love this guy," she told Hope. "It's been so hard to know he was unhappy all these years." She shrugged. "So, to know that you're happy now," she nodded at Chance, "it's just awesome. Anyway, how about I stop embarrassing us all? Are you here to ride?"

Chance shrugged. "We'd like to, if you can fit us in? I wanted to come see you and introduce you to Hope, but yeah, we'd love to ride out, if it's possible."

Lily nodded and beckoned for them to come into the camper with her. "Of course. We'll figure something out. We're busy with weekend lessons, but it's mostly kids, so some of the bigger horses are free. I just need to check who's available. "I'm teaching a class in half an hour, so I can't take you out, but it's not as if you need me, is it?"

Chance shook his head. "Not if you're cool with turning us loose."

Lily laughed. "Not a problem at all. I know you're more capable of taking care of Hope and the horses than anyone else—even me. And I'm sure you'd rather go by yourselves."

She ran her finger down the page of a big diary on the desk, then looked up at Hope. "How much riding have you done?"

"Some. I grew up riding, but it's been a while."

Chance nodded. "She's good enough in the saddle."

"Okay." Lily looked back at the list. "I know exactly who I can put you on, Chance. Archie, he's new around here and he's a bit of a handful, but only because he's young and willful. I'd love for you to take him out and let me know what you think."

Chance smiled. "Sounds good to me."

"And for you, Hope, I'm not sure. We have Bessie, who will take very good care of you, but is very steady."

Chance chuckled. "You mean a plod along?"

Lily smiled. "Yes. She's a great teacher, but it won't be a thrill ride. Or we have another mare who's a real sweetie. She's sweet and kind, but she runs like the wind."

Hope looked at Chance. She liked the sound of that, but wanted to know what he thought.

"Is she easy enough to stop?"

"Absolutely," said Lily. "I wouldn't offer her if she had any vices. She's great, as long as you can handle a good gallop?"

Hope nodded. "I think I can, but I'll defer to the master. What do you think?"

Chance nodded. "You'll probably enjoy yourself more than you would with a plod along."

"Okay," said Lily. "Faith it is."

Hope raised an eyebrow, not understanding. "Excuse me?"

"That's her name, Faith."

Chance groaned. "Seriously?"

Hope laughed. "I guess I'll just have to call you, love."

Chance shook his head with a sigh and looked at Lily. "Can you imagine what it's like to be called Chance and Hope?"

"I think it's awesome. It's like you were meant to be. And now you have Faith as well."

"Yeah, yeah, all right."

Hope liked Lily. She worked quickly and efficiently, and the stables seemed to run like clockwork. There were two lessons going on, and Lily glanced over occasionally to check on them. It seemed that all the kids were having fun and the instructors were great. It wasn't long before Archie and Faith were standing in the yard, saddled up and ready to go.

Lily checked her watch. "I'm going to have to get ready for my lesson in a minute. Are you good with everything?" she asked Chance. "Do you remember the trails? Have any questions for me?"

"No, I'm fine. Don't worry. It's all good. I'll take care of Faith, Hope, and Archie," he said with a rueful smile.

Lily laughed. "Okay then. Just one more thing. Get your phone out and save my number. You can call me if you need anything."

Once that was done, she stood back and smiled at Hope. "Have fun out there. You've got the best trail leader and probably the best horse."

Hope smiled back. "Thanks so much for this. When do you need us back?"

Lily shrugged. "Whenever you like. Two hours is the usual trail ride. You can follow the loop out by Jackson Creek, but it's up to you. Just do me a favor and call if you're going to be more than two hours so I don't start worrying?"

"I'll tell you now, we'll be back in two hours, but we're going to take the Hidden Valley trail."

Lily smiled. "Of course, you are. I should have known. In that case I'll see you around eleven-thirty."

Hope stroked Faith's neck as they set out following Chance and Archie up a narrow trail that led away from the barn and up into the hills. "It's nice to meet you, Faith." She spoke quietly to the horse and watched her ears flick back and forth to listen. "I'm Hope, and I'll be the one up here trying not to interfere, too much, okay?"

Faith nodded her head as if she understood, and Hope chuckled to herself.

Chance turned in his saddle as Archie pranced ahead. "Are you two okay back there?"

"We're great. We're just getting to know each other."

He smiled and turned back around as Archie lunged to one side. Hope knew she would have fallen off if Faith made a move like that, but Chance moved with Archie as if they were one. She could hear him talking, though she couldn't make out the words, just a low comforting sound that seemed to calm Archie down.

The trail widened after a while, and Hope urged Faith forward so she could ride alongside Chance. He smiled at her. "How are you doing?"

She nodded. "Great. I like her, and I think she likes me."

"How could she not?" he asked with a grin.

"How about you; is he okay?" Archie seemed like a handful to her, though Chance didn't seem worried.

He nodded. "He's a good kid, he's just a youngster and he wants to play. Lily's going to have her hands full if she wants to turn him into a riding school horse."

"I like him, but I wish Hercules were here."

Chance raised an eyebrow. "You do?"

"I do, don't you?"

"Yeah, I've been thinking that all morning. There was just something special about that guy."

"You really liked him, didn't you?"

"I did. I even thought about going back to get him, but it wouldn't be right."

"Why not?"

"He's not a cow horse. He's a fun horse. Most of my saddle time is work. I don't get to ride just for fun. It wouldn't be fair to him, he's better off where he is."

"I was kind of hoping that you might find time to ride for fun more now."

His head jerked up and he met her gaze. "Shit! Of course. I'm sorry. I guess I haven't gotten used to the fact that you're there now. I'm not saying I don't want to ride out with you. I just didn't think."

"That's okay, I know."

They rode on in silence. Chance looked thoughtful and she wondered if he was reconsidering about Hercules.

The trail opened into a wide meadow and Archie started to prance. "Do you want to let them go?"

Hope nodded. "I'm looking forward to finding out what Lily meant about her running like the wind."

Chance pressed his lips together. "How about we find out what cantering in circles is like first?"

Hope laughed. "You don't trust me in the saddle yet, do you?"

He shook his head. "It's Faith I don't trust."

"Aww." Hope patted her neck. "She's a sweetheart."

"She sure seems it, but when it comes to horses, trust needs to be earned, not just given. Let me watch you canter her around up there." He pointed to a big, flat grassy area.

"Yes, boss." She saluted him then trotted Faith away and put her through her paces. She was a great ride. She had a long floaty stride that made Hope feel like she was riding on air. She responded immediately to everything Hope asked of her.

"Okay, I'm a believer," called Chance. "Just let me do a little work with this guy?"

He urged Archie forward and Hope watched what seemed to be a power struggle between them with Archie prancing and lunging and Chance keeping him under a tight rein. After a few minutes, Hope laughed when Archie seemed to accept who was in charge. He dropped his head and arched his neck and trotted forward. "Do you think that's why he's called Archie?"

Chance smiled. "Knowing Lily, it probably is." He rode back to join her. "Okay, now we know what we're dealing with, do you want to go up to the top of the meadow?"

Hope nodded eagerly. "Can we gallop?"

"Not this first time. I want to get a feel for the land. I don't want to go tearing up there and have one of them loose their leg in a hole."

"Okay." She loved that he was cautious when it came to the horses. She didn't think of him as a cautious man, but he certainly looked out for the horses—and for her. She wondered if he'd have just galloped on if she weren't with him. He urged Archie forward and Faith followed, catching Hope unaware. She shifted in the saddle and righted herself and asked Faith to slow. Hope relaxed when she did; she'd been a little concerned that she might not be able to stop her. Feeling more confident, she gave Faith her head and cantered on after Chance. She loved riding out with him and she loved even more that this was going to be a part of her life now. A part of their life.

When they rode back into the yard at the stables, Lily came out of the camper and greeted them with a smile. "How did it go?"

Chance nodded. "Great. This guy," he slid down from Archie and patted his neck, "is going to turn out to be a fine horse, but I'm not sure he's ever going to be a school horse."

Lily nodded. "I had a feeling you might say that. He's a sweetie, but I've been thinking it'd almost be a shame to keep him here. He's not quite the right temperament, is he? I think he'd be bored in this life. I don't suppose you'd have any use for him, would you?"

Chance shook his head sadly. "He's not right for my kind of work." He pursed his lips. "He could be, maybe. I dunno. Let me think about it?"

"Of course."

"What about Faith?" asked Chance as Hope dismounted and rubbed the mare's nose.

"What about her?" asked Lily.

"She's one I could find a use for."

Hope turned around to look at him. She hadn't thought Faith was like the horses he used to work the herd. He narrowed his eyes at her and smiled.

Lily mulled it over. "I'd hate to lose her."

"She's a good un," agreed Chance. "But we both know she'd be happier in Montana."

Lily laughed. "That's not fair. You're going to ask me to sell her so she'll be happier?"

Chance nodded. "Of course, I am. I drive a hard a bargain and appealing to your better nature isn't going to hurt my bargaining power."

Lily sighed. "Then I'll say the same as you did. Let me think about it?"

"Sure."

Hope rubbed Faith's nose, hoping that Lily would say yes, and Faith would end up in Montana. She was a beautiful horse and Hope was already attached to her

"What are you two doing this afternoon?" asked Lily.

Hope's heart sank. Chance had been relaxed and happy, but she sensed a change in him at the question. Would he tell Lily that he was going to the cemetery?

"We need to get going," he said. "You can imagine how many people we have to catch up with."

Lily smiled, seeming to sense that she shouldn't have asked. "I'll bet. Well, if I don't see you before you leave, at least give me a call? Let me know what you're thinking about Archie and Faith?"

"Sure, and thanks again, Lil."

"Nate and I are going to the Boathouse tonight. Everyone's meeting up. Do you think you might drop in?"

Chance nodded. "Maybe."

Lily smiled at Hope. "It was so nice to meet you."

"You, too."

Chapter Nine

Chance walked down Main toward the bakery. He'd arranged to meet Renée there so that he could leave the rental car with Hope. He could walk around town and get someone to give him a ride anywhere he wanted to go. He didn't like the idea of her being stranded without transport if she wanted to go back to the cabin, or anywhere else.

He hesitated outside the bakery. Renée had bought the place from Ben and had taken over the adjoining building, too, so she could open a women's center. He wasn't too clear on what the women's center did, other than provide help and advice to women who needed it. He looked up at the sign over the door, then closed his eyes and blew out a sigh. The sign read, Chloe's Place. He'd come up with the name himself. Renée had been about to call it Summer Lake Women's Center and that just hadn't sounded right to Chance. It sounded more like some institution—a place women would rather stay away from. He'd told Renée it needed to sound welcoming, a friendly place where the women would feel comfortable and safe. Seeing the sign made him catch his breath, but he liked it; it made him feel proud.

He peered through the window of the bakery and saw both Renée and April standing there watching him. He smiled. He had a lot of time for both of them. He pushed open the door and greeted them with a smile. "Ladies."

"Chance!" Renée came around the counter and wrapped him in a hug. "How are you? Where is she?"

"Can you wait a minute before you start with all the questions?" April came to hug him, too. "I have to go. I need to pick Marcus up, but I waited to see you first."

"I'm glad you did. How's things? Is Eddie being good to you?"

April blushed and nodded. "Very good. He's an amazing man, Chance. I hope one of these days you'll have time to get to know him better."

Chance nodded. "Yeah, I'd like that."

"You don't have to worry about her, though," said Renée. "I can vouch for that. Eddie's like the perfect husband. He dotes on her and on Marcus."

"Husband?" He looked at April. "You got married?"

"No, I still don't have my divorce through yet."

"But once it's final, you can bet she'll be married in no time. Eddie's waiting, not so patiently."

Chance smiled. "You take your time and make sure it's right for you."

"It is. He is. And it's all thanks to you, Chance. If you and Mason hadn't gotten me out of Montana ..." She shuddered.

"Hey." He put a hand on her shoulder. "All that's behind you. You need to forget about it, and get on with being happy now you've got the chance."

"Wise words," said Renée. He turned to meet her gaze and she nodded slightly.

April sensed the tension between them and hugged Chance again. "I really have to go. I hope I'll see you before you leave. I'd love to meet Hope."

He nodded. "We might drop into the Boathouse tonight. Will you be there?"

"Yes. Eddie's playing and Marcus is staying at Ethan's tonight. So, I'll see you there."

Chance nodded. He hadn't said he and Hope were going, but maybe they would.

Once she'd gone, he turned back to Renée. "What did you mean when you said they were wise words?"

Renée pulled the cap off her head and pushed her wild hair back when it sprang free. "You know damned well what I meant." She smiled to soften the words. "You don't see the irony in what you said to April?"

He nodded grudgingly and she smiled. "If someone, anyone, even I, had said those words to you not so long ago, you would have gone all silent and broody and disappeared for another couple of months, wouldn't you?"

The smile that came to his lips surprised him. "Yeah, you're right."

"Wow. You really have come a long way since you met Hope, haven't you?"

He nodded. "She's good for me, Renée."

"I can see that and I hope to God you understand that I am truly happy for you."

Chance had to swallow around the lump in his throat. "I think I do, but I still feel guilty as hell. I feel like I'm cheating on Chloe." He swiped angrily at the tears that welled up in his eyes.

"Oh, Chance." Renée's eyes filled with tears, too, and she put a hand on his arm. "You mustn't feel that way. Chloe's not here. She can't give you the love and happiness you deserve. Hope can."

He nodded and cleared his throat. "I know, and she does. I want to be with her. I want to ask her to marry me, but I need to know that's okay with you."

Renée shook her head adamantly. "Excuse my language, but that's fucked up!"

He couldn't help but chuckle. He hadn't heard Renée use that word before.

"It is, Chance! God, I hope you can see how fucked up that really is?" Renée wasn't laughing.

"I can. I know, but it's how I feel. You and me, we've been the only ones keeping Chloe here."

"No. We haven't. She's not here. She's dead, Chance."

The tears welled up again, but he was grateful to her for ramming the truth home so hard.

"Chloe's dead and gone." Her voice was gentler as she went on. "And to use your own wise words against you, it's like you just told April. All that's behind you. You need to forget about it, and get on with being happy now you've got the chance."

He nodded. "I know, and I am doing. I came here thinking that I wanted your blessing to move on, but you've made me realize something."

"And what's that?"

"It's not your blessing I'm looking for. It's something more real than that. I don't want me being with Hope to mean that I have to lose you. You and me, we're like family, because we thought we were going to be family. I don't want that to change."

She smiled and pushed her hair away from her face. "I don't either, but it might have to change between us." She waved her finger at him as he started to interrupt. "Hope has to be your number one priority, and I can't imagine how she would feel."

Chance smiled. "You'd never guess how she feels. She wants to meet you, if you want to. She's amazing, Renée. She understands. I think she understands better than I do. She's the one who made me understand that I don't have to give Chloe up. That Chloe will always be a part of me."

Renée wiped her eyes and smiled. "Wow, she sounds pretty amazing, and yes, I'd love to meet her. I'll go with whatever the two of you want. Part of me has been preparing myself to back out of your life. You've got a new future ahead of you."

"No! I don't want you to do that. Please? It's like Hope says, Chloe is a part of me, you are a part of me. I still want you to be a part of the future. Mine and Hope's future."

She nodded. "I didn't say I don't want to. I just want to do whatever's best for you."

"I know. You're the best."

"Glad you remembered. But promise me something?"

Chance's blood ran cold. The last promise he'd ever made was to Renée. She'd made him promise that he wouldn't go after Chloe and Kyle that night, that he'd wait until the morning.

"Are you okay? You've gone white."

He sucked in a deep breath then slowly blew it out before he answered. "I don't do promises, not anymore."

Renée covered her face with her hand for a moment, then slowly lowered it. "I'm sorry."

He nodded. "So am I."

"Don't you think it's time you moved past that?" He narrowed his eyes at her, but she just shook her head at him. "You don't intimidate me, not anymore. I care too much about you. If you and Hope are going to have a future, I imagine you're planning to make her a promise?"

"I don't do promises," he repeated.

"So, what are we doing? Are we splitting hairs and claiming that vows are somehow different from promises? You do want to marry her, right?"

"I do."

"Yeah, well those two words right there are the most important promise you will ever make."

He nodded. She was right. Even though he hadn't thought of it like that until now.

"Okay. You know how sorry I am that I made you promise me that night. But I've made my peace with it. Now you need to do the same. Do you think that's possible?"

Chance rolled it around in his mind and was surprised at what he found. He met her gaze. "I think I already have. I don't blame you, I never did. I blamed myself for years, but now that I really think about it, I don't believe that promise affected anything. Even if I hadn't promised you, we don't know what might have happened. Chloe might still have died."

Renée nodded. "Even if that promise was the thing that killed her—and I don't believe it made any difference at all—but even if it was, it's time we both let it go."

"You're right. Since I met Hope I've been reexamining everything that I think, everything that I feel about what happened. And I'm finding that I don't really believe any of it anymore. I've just clung to it all like a bunch of old superstitions."

Renée smiled. "That's a good way to describe it. That's what I did, too. But Chance, it's time to let it all go. It's time to be happy."

He nodded. "I am."

"Good. Now, I know you and Gabe want to meet up, so do you want to come up to the house?"

Chance was about to automatically refuse. Renée still lived in the house where she and Chloe grew up. The house where he and Chloe had spent so much time when they were teenagers. He hadn't been up there since she died. Renée raised an eyebrow and waited. He shrugged.

"Maybe I should."

"Maybe, but not if you don't want to. And where's Hope? What's she doing?"

"She's having lunch with Miss."

"Okay. As long as you haven't left her sitting somewhere by herself."

He chuckled. "As she told me, she's a big girl. She wanted to get to know Missy better and she wants to explore the town, too. She likes it here."

"Do you think you'd ever move back?"

"No. My life is there now. It's where Hope grew up, too."

Renée smiled. "I'm glad you found such a good place, with such good people."

"Me too. I don't know what would have happened to me if it weren't for Dave Remington. I was on a bad path till he came along."

"All you can do is be grateful that he did, and make the best of what you have now. Come on. Gabe's home and he's been going through that contract you sent one more time. He thinks Seymour Davenport must be your biggest fan. He was expecting to find all kinds of tricks and sneaky clauses, but it sounds as though it's all written in your favor."

Chance nodded. "I was surprised, but Seymour's a good guy, and he seems to think I'm a good guy."

"Then he's a good judge of character as well as a genius billionaire," said Renée with a smile as she led him out of the bakery and locked up behind them.

~ ~ ~

Missy put down her fork and wrinkled her nose. "So, what do you think? Do you think you can put up with us?"

Hope laughed. "I think I love you! And I love your dad and Alice. Your Dan's a real sweetheart and Scot's a great kid."

Missy nodded. "I think so, but it must be weird for you. Don't take offense, will you, hon? But I doubt we're anything like what you're used to. I will admit that when I first found out that you and Chance were seeing each other in Oregon, I went online and dug up everything I could find about you. You've had a very different life than Chance. I mean, that actor, Drew … whatever his name is? I can see you being with someone like that, someone who moves in the same circles and has boatloads of money, but Chance isn't like that."

Hope shook her head. She'd enjoyed her lunch with Missy, but had felt she was holding back a little. It seemed she'd finally gotten to what was really on her mind. "Chance is nothing like that, and that's what I love about him. Yes, I come from a different world. My life hasn't been normal, but now I'm back in Montana and I'm becoming a part of Chance's life and I love it. The Remingtons are such wonderful people. It must have helped you, knowing that he was with them, even though he wasn't here."

Missy shrugged and looked out at the lake. "Not really. I've never met them."

"Oh! I'm sorry. I didn't realize. I assumed …"

Missy smiled. "It's okay. He needed to keep his two worlds separate, and I think I understand that. He never wanted me to go up there. He used to make excuses before, when I was single, about not wanting me around a bunch of cowboys. Then I met Dan and he kept saying he'd invite us when he had some free time, but he never did." She shrugged again. "I don't know what he thinks is going to happen when the two of you get married, but I'm telling you right now, I want to be there."

Hope nodded. She still felt a little uncomfortable with all this talk about when they got married.

"And I wanted to apologize for yesterday, too. I shouldn't have put you both on the spot like that—asking if he'd even proposed yet."

"That's okay. We'll get there in our own time. We haven't really known each other that long. I think we both knew fairly early on that we wanted to be together, but we didn't know if we were capable of it."

Missy gave her an inquiring look.

"I mean, Chance didn't know if he had it in him to love anyone who wasn't Chloe, and even loving someone isn't always enough. You still have to figure out if and how you can have them in your life."

Missy nodded. "But you've figured it out now?"

"I hope so. We've overcome a lot of hurdles."

"I think the two of you will make it, I really do. You're good for him."

Hope smiled.

"Is he good for you?"

She nodded.

"How?"

"He's a good man. He's real. He makes me feel safe, not just safe, but like I've found where I belong in the world. He's my place to be. He's the first person in my life who I know is always going to be there for me." She frowned, wanting to explain that better. "I don't mean that in a mushy romantic way." She smiled. "Well, I suppose I do, but it's more than that, too. He's got my back. Even if we weren't together anymore I know that Chance is the kind of man I could turn to and he would always be there. It's who he is. He's solid. He's a man of his word ..." She shrugged. "I'm rambling. I don't know how to put it any better."

"You don't need to. You explained it perfectly. You see who he is and you love him for it. That's all I needed to know."

Hope smiled. "I'm glad you like me. I think you'd be a tough sister to deal with if you didn't."

Missy laughed. "Who said I like you?"

Hope laughed with her. "I did, and don't try and make out that you don't. I've won you over and we both know it."

Missy grinned. "You have and the fact that you'll talk to me like that reassures me that you won't take any crap from Chance either."

"I won't, at least not stupid crap. I try to help him through the emotional stuff; we all have some of that to deal with, and he has more than most."

"I'd say you've helped him past most of it, and I love you for it. Thank you."

Hope nodded.

"Do you want to get out of here?" asked Missy. They were still sitting at a table on the deck of the Boathouse where they'd had lunch.

Hope got up gratefully. "Yeah, my butt's going numb, these picnic benches aren't the most comfortable, are they?"

Missy laughed. "You should tell Ben that, but if you're going to be spending any time here at the lake, I think you'll just have to get used to them."

"What do you want to do?" asked Missy as they walked across the parking lot. "Do you want to come back to my place, or do you want me to take you on a tour of the town or something?"

Hope thought about it. She quite liked the idea of wandering around the town by herself, getting to know the place, but she didn't want to pass up the chance to spend time with Missy. "How about you give me that tour."

"Perfect. In that case we can leave the cars here and just walk down Main Street."

As they set off, Hope couldn't help smiling to herself. She felt at home here and now she felt as though she had another new friend who would hopefully soon become a sister. Her smile faded a little. Missy and the girls up in Montana would only become her family if Chance ever asked her to marry him. They'd started to talk about their life as if marriage were a foregone conclusion. She believed it was, but a little part of her was starting to hope that he'd get on and propose to her soon.

Chapter Ten

Chance jumped up from his seat on the deck when he heard a car pull up outside the cabin. He'd been back a while and was starting to get a little concerned about Hope, even though he knew he shouldn't. He could have called her if he really wanted, but he'd resisted, preferring instead to let her do her own thing and come back when she was ready. He'd gone with Renée up to her place to see Gabe. He'd been tense on the drive up there, concerned that it would be hard to revisit that place and all the memories it held. It hadn't been like that. The old house was gone. Renée told him that they'd torn it down before it fell down. The place they'd built was beautiful and gave Chance a few ideas about what he'd like to do when he and Hope built a place. Gabe had given him another idea, too; he'd joked that Renée had made him live in the crumbly old house for far too long because she was too proud to let him buy or build her a new one. Renée had reminded him that she didn't have a penny after her ex was arrested for defrauding the charity they both ran. She hadn't wanted Gabe to spend a million on a house that she couldn't contribute to. It turned out that she had been able to contribute though. She owned the land where her family house had stood and as the market had recovered, it was a very valuable lot. In the end, she'd put up the land and Gabe had put up the house. Chance loved it. It made him feel that he could do right by Hope, after all. He should let her build as much house as she wanted; he could contribute the land they built it on.

He hurried inside and met Hope just as she was letting herself in through the front door.

"Oh, hey. I didn't think you'd be back yet."

"I've been back a while. How was your afternoon?"

She grinned. "Missy and I had a great time. I think we're going to become good friends."

"I'm going to need to watch myself then."

"Yep. Anyway, how was your afternoon?"

He nodded. "It was good, better than I expected."

They went through to the kitchen and he poured them both a lemonade. "Do you want to come sit outside for a while and tell me about your day?"

"Okay." She followed him out and took a seat. "I can't get enough of this view. It's almost as good as sitting out on the back porch of the cabin looking at the mountains."

"It is. I love that view, but I love this one as well."

"Would you ever want to move back here?"

"I don't know. Renée asked me that this afternoon and I automatically said no. I've never thought it was an option. I never wanted to. Plus, I've got even more reason to stay in the valley now."

"You do? Why's that?"

He narrowed his eyes at her. "Hmm, let me think what it was again. Oh yeah, I remember. I met this chick and she grew up there. She just moved back and so did her dad. Even if I wanted to move away—which I don't—it wouldn't be fair to ask her to."

"Maybe it would be fairer to ask her, than to just decide for her. She might love it here."

"Seriously?"

She shrugged. "Not really. At least I don't think so. I do love it here, but like you said, I just moved back to Montana, and I love it. And Dad's there too now, it'd hardly be fair to move away. But," she stared out at the lake for a few moments, then looked back at him. "maybe we could have a vacation home here?"

Chance pressed his lips together. He was finally managing to wrap his head around the fact that he should let her pay for as much home as she wanted, and here she was suggesting they should have two! "Maybe."

She held his gaze for a moment and he could tell she knew what he was thinking. "I don't mean right away. We're going to need some time to get used to everything, to each other and to our life in Montana, but maybe in a year or two it'll seem like a good idea. It'd be nice to do it while …" She stopped herself short and he had a nasty feeling he knew what she'd been about to say—while your dad's still around. "We don't need to worry about it yet. A more pressing question is whether you want to go out tonight. You know Missy wants us to go."

He nodded. "I know. I've been thinking we should, if you want to."

"I'd like to, but I don't want that to feel like pressure on you. If you don't want to go then I'm sure we can think of something to do right here." She came around and sat in his lap, wrapping her arms around his neck and nibbling his bottom lip.

His arms closed around her and pulled her closer. She felt so good with her soft warm body pressed against his—especially her soft warm ass pressed against his now hard cock. "Maybe we should do both?" He slid his hand inside her top and pushed the cup of her bra aside. He loved her plump, soft breasts, and loved the way her nipples tightened into hard peaks whenever he touched her.

She sighed. "Yes, please."

He smiled and rolled her nipple between his finger and thumb, making her gasp. "Right now?"

She nodded and ground her ass against him. "Right now."

"Right here?"

Her eyes widened and she looked at him and then all around them. "You mean, right here? Out here?"

He nodded and shifted his hand to her legs, pushing her skirt up around her thighs. "I do."

She looked excited at the prospect. "Do you think it's okay?"

"Yeah. There's no one around. These cabins are set up to be completely private." Even as he said it, he got a bad feeling and stopped himself, just before his fingers found their way inside her panties. "But you're right, we should probably take it inside, just to be safe."

"Oh." She looked so disappointed it was comical. "But ..."

He shook his head. "We can't get reckless, just because the press has left you alone since Matt, it doesn't mean they've forgotten you completely. It would be just my luck for someone to snap some photos of us going at it out here."

She laughed. "Going at it?"

He nodded and let go of her so they could get up. "Yep. I'm going to take you inside right now and we're going to go at it like bunnies."

She laughed again. "You mad romantic fool, you."

He shrugged. "I never claimed to be one of those." As he took her by the hand and led her inside he sensed a tension that hadn't been there before. She wasn't laughing anymore. Did she want him to be more romantic? His mind went straight back to the fact that he hadn't asked her to marry him yet. He hadn't done it because he wanted to come up with something that was romantic, but was also him. He couldn't think of anything that would fit both. He stopped when they got to the kitchen. He didn't want to take her to bed when she seemed to have lost her excitement. He turned to her and smiled. "Do you want to save it for later, when we get back?"

She nodded. "Maybe we should."

~ ~ ~

Chance took hold of her hand when they got close to the Boathouse. The place looked to be packed. There was a band set up outside on the deck and most of the tables were taken already.

"Are you ready for this?" he asked.

"I am, are you?"

"Yeah. I'm kind of looking forward to it."

"That's good."

"It is. This, you and me, us being here together, it feels right."

Hope smiled, but didn't say anything. Part of her had been worried that once he came back here, he'd feel that he couldn't be with her, but the opposite seemed to be true. He confirmed that with his next words.

"It might have taken me a long time to get over Chloe, but I'm glad it did. I know now, especially after talking to Renée today that, not only am I ready to move on, but I already have moved on."

Hope looked up at him.

He nodded and squeezed her hand. "I told Renée this afternoon that I feel like everything I've clung to about Chloe and me was just a bunch of superstitions I built up. Chloe's gone. I wasn't trying to hold on to her, even though I thought I was. I was just trying to hold on to my feelings for her." He looked down at her and dropped a kiss on her lips. "My feelings for her were the feelings of an eighteen-year-old kid. My feelings for you are so much more than that."

Hope's eyes filled with tears.

He shook his head. "Don't cry, honey. You should be happy. I am. I'm happy that I've finally figured it out. I was a kid back then. Now I'm a man and you've helped me become a better man. I want to keep getting better and become the best man I can be, for you."

"You're the best man I've ever known."

"I want to be. I love you, Hope."

"I love you."

"Hey, Chance!"

They both looked up to see Pete Hemming coming across the square with a woman Hope assumed must be his wife.

Chance squeezed her hand and spoke quietly out the side of his mouth. "And so, it begins. I'll warn you now, if I reach my limit I might just grab you and hightail it out of here. And if you reach your limit, you should do the same. Okay?"

"Deal."

"Hey, Pete. Holly."

"I'm glad you came," said Pete. "Hope, I'd like to introduce you to my wife, Holly."

Hope shook hands with Holly. "It's nice to meet you. You seem familiar for some reason."

Holly smiled. "We've never met, but we've been at a few of the same fashion shows over the years. I own a boutique in LA …"

"Hayes!" exclaimed Hope. "Oh, wow! You're Holly Hayes."

"I am."

Pete grinned at Chance. "I suggest we get them inside before we let them start talking. Otherwise we'll be standing out here all night."

"Watch it, Bigshot." Hope laughed as Holly slapped Pete's butt. "How about you go get us a drink while we talk and then you come find us with it?"

"Yes, ma'am, anything you say, ma'am." Pete looked at Chance. "Come on, you'll get used to being dismissed by the womenfolk. We'll probably find some of the guys at the bar already."

Hope caught his eye. She hated for the moment they'd just shared to be broken up this way. She was worried that he might not want to go with Pete and possibly be dragged into a big group conversation with the other guys. But he winked at her and smiled. "Are you okay?"

She nodded. She was used to networking with women in the fashion industry. She wasn't worried for herself, just for him. "I'm fine. I'm sure Holly and I will have plenty to talk about."

"You can say that again, girlfriend," said Holly and slipped her arm through Hope's. "Let's go find a quiet corner so I can have you to myself for a minute before everyone realizes you're here and descends on you."

Hope looked back over her shoulder at Chance as Holly led her through the bar. He turned back too and they smiled at each other. That helped. It made her feel that whatever they were about to be subjected to individually, they were at least united in the face of it.

Holly slid into an empty booth in a quiet corner and Hope sat down opposite her. "Sorry I dragged you away like that, but I just have to tell you how much I adore your clothes."

"Thank you, but I can't really take the credit for them. We hired a couple of young designers last year and they're the ones coming up with the great new stuff."

Holly waved her hand. "Don't be so modest, you've been designing the best workout gear there is for years."

"Thanks. What about you? Do you have your own label?"

"No. I'm not a designer. I know great clothes when I see them, but I can't come up with them myself." Holly looked up. "Uh-oh, it doesn't look like I'll get you to myself for long, here come Missy and Emma."

Hope looked around. She was curious to meet Emma after what her husband had said yesterday.

"What are you two up to?" asked Missy. "I thought everyone was meeting out on the deck?"

"We are," said Holly with a smile, "but I took the most of the opportunity to get Hope to myself for a minute."

Emma laughed. "Well, sorry, but your minute's up." She smiled at Hope. "Hi, I'm Emma. I believe you met my husband, Jack, yesterday."

Hope made to shake hands with her, but Emma slid into the booth beside her and wrapped her in a hug. "Sorry. I'm a hugger. I'm sure everyone's told you how nice it is to meet you, but I am soooo happy to meet you. I really am."

Hope couldn't help but like her. "Thank you."

"No, thank you! Poor Chance has been so sad for so long, and now he's finally happy and it's all down to you. I think you're my new favorite person."

Hope laughed. Chance wasn't joking when he'd said Emma was a sweetheart.

Missy slid in next to Holly. "Don't mind our Em, you'll get used to her. I'm just glad she's not scratching your eyes out."

"Missy!" Emma's cheeks were bright red and Hope felt bad for her. "I'm not like that." She met Hope's gaze. "I'm sure someone's about to tell you, if they haven't already, that I have a teeny crush on Chance."

Holly and Missy laughed loudly. "Make that a huge crush that she's had for at least twenty years."

Emma hung her head and Hope put a hand on her arm, wanting to make her feel better. "Well, if anyone understands that it's me. I had a crush on him the minute I met him. We just have good taste in men, don't we? Your Jack's a hottie, to say the least."

Emma smiled at her. "I think so."

Hope made a face at Missy. "You don't understand because he's your brother, that's all."

Emma nodded. "See, I've been telling you that for years. Hope gets it."

Chance and Pete arrived at the booth. "Sorry ladies," said Pete. "We only got Holly and Hope a drink."

"That's okay," said Missy. "Jack and Dan got ours, they're outside on the deck. Are you coming?"

Hope looked up at Chance. He was smiling and didn't seem uncomfortable. He raised an eyebrow and she nodded. So far, she liked everyone she'd met. She was looking forward to meeting the others.

~ ~ ~

Once they were seated outside, Chance looked around at everyone. They'd had to pull three of the big picnic benches together to accommodate everyone. That made him smile. He remembered when people had started moving back here and Missy had been so happy about it. He'd come for her birthday a couple of years ago and at that point their gang of friends had all fit at one picnic bench. It made him wonder if he and Hope might come to live here one day, like so many others had.

He rested his hand on Hope's knee beneath the table. He wasn't sure if she'd like him keeping his arm around her in front of everyone, but he wanted her to know he was watching out for her.

She turned and smiled at him.

"Are you okay with this?"

She nodded. "I am. I'm having fun. Are you?"

"Yeah." He smiled realizing that he was having fun. He raised a hand when he spotted Gabe and Renée making their way out onto the deck. Hope had said she wanted to meet them. He hoped she still felt that way. "Are you sure you're okay with meeting Renée?"

"I'm looking forward to it. Is that her?"

"Yeah." He was about to get up to introduce them, but Hope beat him to it. She got to her feet and went to greet Renée before she reached the picnic table. Chance scrambled after her.

"Hi. I'm Hope."

Renée smiled. "I know."

Chance watched the two women standing there facing each other for a long awkward moment. He wanted to do something, say something, to break the silence, but he couldn't. He just stood there transfixed, feeling as though he was watching his past come face to face with his future. He knew everyone else had stopped talking and was watching. He felt like his fate hung in the balance, as if the outcome of this encounter would define how he moved forward in life. He thought Hope moved first, but it might have been Renée. He didn't know; it didn't matter. All that mattered was that they both stepped forward and hugged each other. There was genuine affection in that embrace. Both women closed their eyes and Chance just knew that they were both hiding tears. He had to swallow and blink a couple of times himself. When they let go of each other, Renée said something he couldn't hear and Hope nodded. They turned and walked away into the crowd.

Gabe met his gaze with a smile. "Do you mind if I join you? Looks like they're going to take a while."

"I hope they do. Come on, let's go to the bar." He'd barely started his drink, and Gabe had a full one in his hand, but Chance needed to escape. He knew all the eyes turned in his direction were filled with concern, but he couldn't stand so much attention focused on him.

Chapter Eleven

Hope woke early on Sunday morning. She lay there running through the events of last night. It had been a great night. Chance's friends were a great bunch of people and she hoped that they'd come back here often. She wanted to get to know them all, especially Renée. When they'd first met, Hope hadn't known what to say, despite having so much she wanted to say. Renée had made it easy. She'd asked Hope if she wanted to come outside with her. They'd walked across the square and sat on a bench on Main Street for a good twenty minutes. By the time they'd gone back into the Boathouse, Hope knew she'd made a friend for life. She didn't want Chance being with her to make him feel that he had to lose touch with Renée, especially since Renée still saw Chance as part of her family. Renée had said she hoped that maybe someday the two of them would see each other as sisters-in-law. That meant a lot and Hope loved the idea.

She smiled as she lay there thinking about Emma. She was so sweet. The others had teased her again later about her crush on Chance. The poor thing blushed like crazy, but Hope had defended her every time. At one point, Emma had told Hope that Jack's mom had a crush on her dad. Jack had rolled his eyes and said that all the women in his life seemed to have a crush on someone. Hope had laughed along with them, but it had made her wonder if her dad might ever find love again, if he'd ever open his heart up to the possibility. She hoped he would.

"Good morning. You look happy."

She rolled on her side and planted a kiss on Chance's nose. He was so sexy, even when he was only half awake. "I am."

"What are you thinking about that's got you smiling so much?"

"Right then I was thinking about Emma and how sweet she is. I was also thinking about Jack's mom having a crush on my dad. It makes me want to introduce them."

Chance shook his head. "I know what you mean, but if he's ever going to let another woman into his life, it'll be a woman he chooses himself, and it'll be in his own time."

"I know. Just like you."

Chance nodded and pulled her closer. "Exactly. I wouldn't have thanked anyone for trying to set me up with someone."

Hope laughed. "I don't imagine you would. You'd probably have gone all broody and disappeared."

"Yup. It's easier to go dark than to stick around when people are interfering in your life—no matter how good their intentions. I feel what I feel and that doesn't change just because someone else thinks it doesn't make sense. No one can talk me into changing my feelings. Not even I can do that. It doesn't work that way. Feelings change with time and by what we live through and what we learn from it."

"I know you're right. I wouldn't try to force Dad into anything, but it's hard not to want to help him toward happiness."

"It is, but the best way to help him is to let him get there in his own time. You need to understand what he feels, not try to change it to what you think he should feel."

"I know."

Chance smiled. "Maybe he'll get as lucky as I did and meet a beautiful, smart, kind, strong woman. Maybe he'll meet the only woman on earth who will make him want to work through his shit and finally break free of grief."

"I hope so."

"So do I."

"I'd like to go and see him when we get home."

"Of course; do you want to invite him for dinner?"

Hope nodded. "Yes, I'd like that. We'll have to get something in, though."

"Yeah, we'll figure something out, but you should call him, see if he wants to."

"I will. And are we going to see your dad again before we go? I thought we'd spend more time with him and Alice while we were here."

"He's coming to Miss's today for a big lunch, remember? I'd like to go, if that's okay with you?"

"Of course, it is. What time does she want us?"

"She said noon so that we can spend a couple of hours with them before we have to get to the airport."

"Great. I'd better get up and have a shower, then."

"What's the rush?"

"No rush. I just don't like wasting time in bed."

"I thought it was only wasted if it was spent talking."

She smiled. "Isn't that what we're doing?"

He smiled and rolled her over onto her back. "Not anymore." His mouth came down on her neck, sending shivers of desire through her. She wrapped her arms and legs around him and bit down on his neck, making him gasp.

"You want to play it like that, huh?"

She smiled. "I do." She ran her nails down his back.

He lifted his head and looked at her through narrowed eyes. "You're a scratcher?"

She shrugged. "Maybe."

"I don't think so."

She chuckled and did it again, harder this time. "Are you sure?"

"Yeah, I am." He took hold of her arms and pinned her wrists above her head. She struggled to free them, but he smirked and held her in a vice-like grip. "No more scratching."

"I'll scratch harder, just as soon as I get free."

"I guess I'm just going to have to hold you there, then." He kept hold of her wrists with one hand and stroked his other over her cheek, then on down her neck and over her breast until he was tormenting her nipple.

"Chance," she breathed.

"Yes, honey?" he asked innocently.

She laughed. "You're going to have to let go of me soon."

"And why's that?"

She rubbed her hips against him. "I still have my panties on."

"That doesn't bother me." His hand found its way between her legs and touched her through the lace, making her moan in anticipation.

"It bothers me; I want them gone."

"Your wish is my command."

Instead of letting go of his grip on her wrists, he hooked his finger inside her panties and pulled them to the side. His hard shaft pushed at her and he smiled. "I can get inside any time I please. I don't need to let you go."

He looked so damned smug; she shook her head at him. "Oh, you think so, do you?" She brought her legs together and blocked him out.

He chuckled. It was such deep, sexy sound, she felt herself getting wet for him, but she kept her knees pressed firmly together. "I don't just think so. I know so." He pressed his knee between hers and pried them apart, spreading her legs easily despite her best efforts. He held her gaze as he moved against her. "Do you want it?"

She nodded breathlessly. This was turning her on more than she could have imagined. He had her wrists pinned to the bed, her legs spread with his knees. He was right, he could be inside her any time he chose and she wanted him to choose right now. "Yes!"

He nodded and thrust his hips hard, making her gasp as he filled her. He still held her wrists in place. As they began to move together, she tried to free them again but he wouldn't let go. He held her there as he moved inside her. She moved with him, completely at his mercy as he carried her away. He felt so good—filling her, stretching her, driving her toward her orgasm. She moaned as she got closer and he picked up his pace. He cried her name as he found his release and his orgasm triggered hers, sending her over the edge and carrying her away on a tidal wave of pleasure. Their bodies moved frantically together and he finally let go of her wrists. She brought her arms up around his back and clung on for the ride.

Eventually, he slumped down and kissed her neck. "I love you."

"I love you. I'll have to try scratching you again sometime soon."

"I won't let you."

She chuckled. "I know."

~ ~ ~

A little while later, they sat sipping their coffee out on the deck. Chance was relaxed and happier than he'd ever been. He sucked in a deep breath at that. Was it true? Happier than he'd ever been? He rolled the thought around in his mind. He'd believed that his happiest days had been those he'd spent with Chloe. He'd believed that he'd never be happy again. He nodded to himself. He'd been wrong. He and Chloe had been happy, he believed they'd still be happy if she were still here, but she wasn't. Hope was. Hope had come into his life and turned it around, turned him around.

She looked over at him. "You look like one of those nodding dogs."

He smiled. "I'm happy, that's all."

She smiled, but didn't say anything.

"Are you?"

"Very."

"What would it take to make you even happier than you are right now?"

She shrugged. "I don't know. I'm happy right here. We could maybe go for a walk before we go to Missy's, if you want?"

"Sure." It seemed she wasn't feeling as philosophical as he was. "Let's go."

As they headed up through the resort, Chance wondered where they should go. He could take her out to the beach. She'd probably like it down there, though it might be busy with people walking their dogs on a Sunday morning. The other path from the resort led out along the old road by the river. Did he want to take her there? He did, which surprised the hell out of him. He and Chloe used to walk out there all the time. He'd walked there by himself for the first time on one of his recent visits.

"Which way do you want to go?" asked Hope when they reached the square.

He pointed out toward the river. "That way."

They walked in silence for a while. Chance's mind was busy, but not in the way he'd feared. He didn't feel like he was betraying Chloe by sharing this place with Hope. He was over that. And now he finally knew that he was over it, his mind was racing ahead. Hope was everything to him. He'd always believed Chloe had been the love of his life. He knew now that Hope was. Chloe had been his first love. Since she'd died he'd only been in love with the memory of her and the thought of the life they could have had. He and Hope had a life, a life they were just beginning together. He wanted to start it out right. He wanted her to be his wife, just as soon as they could make it happen. But first he'd have to ask her. He wondered if he should ask her right now, just go down on one knee right here. No. He didn't have a ring or anything. He wanted to ask Seymour's permission first. And although his motive for wanting to do it here was to prove that she was more important to him now than Chloe, that wasn't right. It should be about the two of them. Thoughts of Chloe should have nothing to do with it.

"I can almost hear the cogs whirring in that mind of yours. Want to tell me what's going on in there?"

He shrugged. How could he tell her? "I'm loving being here with you. I'm thinking about getting to spend the rest of our lives together, thinking that maybe we should have a place here so we can come visit."

She nodded. "I'd like that. Do you think it'll help you feel close to Chloe?"

"No!" He took hold of her hand and stopped walking, turning her to face him. "What I was really thinking is about how you're more important to me than Chloe ever really was."

Her eyes widened.

He nodded. "It's true. I loved her. A part of me will always love her, but we were kids. You and me, we're different. What we have is the real deal. We've both lived and loved and lost already. We have some life under our belts and we're going into this as adults. The man I am now loves you in a way that the kid I was back then wasn't capable of understanding, let alone feeling." He slid his arms around her waist and drew her to him. "I love you, Hope, with all my heart and soul. I want us to be together for the rest of our lives. The difference is, I know now that there are no guarantees. I know how precious life is and how it can be over in an instant. I want to make the most of every single moment we get together."

Her eyes filled with tears. "I love you, Chance. I want to spend the rest of my life loving you."

"And we will." He wondered again if he should just ask her to marry him right here and now, but he didn't have a damned ring. If he had, he would've done. He wondered if he could find a minute before they left to go and see Laura. He didn't know the first thing about jewelry, but Laura designed it. He could ask her for the most expensive engagement ring she had.

~ ~ ~

When they got to Missy's, Chance turned and smiled at Hope before he got out of the car. "We don't have to stay too long if you don't want."

"I do want. I told you I want to spend time with them. I told Randy we'd be at the airport and ready to go by two-thirty. That way, we can stop in to see Dad on our way back down the valley. He said he wasn't up for dinner, but he'd love us to stop in for a quick hello. That gives us a good couple of hours here. Unless you want to leave earlier?"

"No. I want to see them."

"Well, so do I. That's one thing you can stop worrying about. I love your family."

He smiled. "They'll be your family too, soon."

"I hope so." She regretted it as soon as she'd said it. She'd snapped at him because he still hadn't asked her to marry him. That was dumb of her and she knew it. He'd ask her when he was ready. There was no big rush. It was only because she'd thought he was going to do it down by the river this morning. For a minute there, she'd really believed that he was about to ask her to marry him. But he hadn't. He gave her a puzzled look, but she shook her head. "Sorry."

At that moment, the front door opened and Missy stood there beckoning them to come in.

Hope smiled and got out of the car, glad that Missy had saved her from having to explain her reaction.

Missy greeted her with a hug and led them through the house and out the back to where Frank and Alice were sitting with Dan.

"There you are," said Frank, starting to get to his feet.

Hope hurried to him and hugged him before he could get up. Alice gave her a grateful smile over his shoulder.

"Sorry we're late."

"You're not," said Frank. "I'm just impatient to see you again; that's all, love. Have you had a good time? What do you think of this little town of ours?"

"I love it." She straightened up and looked at Chance, wondering if she should mention the possibility of them buying a place here.

Chance shook his head. He was probably right. She could only imagine how impatient Frank might get waiting for them to do that.

"She fits right in," said Missy with a smile. "Everyone loves her."

"Why wouldn't they?" asked Frank with a grin.

Chance hugged his dad and then Alice. "No one loves her as much as I do."

Missy smiled at Hope. "Do you want to come help me in the kitchen?"

Hope nodded and followed her back inside. "What do you want me to do?"

Missy laughed and poured two glasses of wine. She handed one to Hope and said, "Just hang with me and drink this. I know you'll have to spend some time with Dad, but I want you to myself for a while, too. How've you enjoyed this weekend?"

"I've loved it. I love the place, I love all your friends. There are so many lovely people I'd like to get to know better."

Missy nodded and lifted the lid off a pan on the stove. She stirred it and then turned back to look at Hope. "I'm glad you like it so much. You're definitely a hit with everyone." She wrinkled her nose and stirred another pan.

"You might as well say whatever it is." Hope knew there was something on her mind.

Missy nodded and gave her a rueful smile. "Okay, I will. How's he been?"

"He's had a great time, too."

Missy sighed. "He did well last night. I was surprised how long the two of you stuck around and how chatty he was."

"He enjoyed himself."

"Good. I guess what I'm worried about is how he's treated you."

Hope frowned. "He …"

Missy shook her head impatiently. "Sorry. I know he treats you well. I guess what I mean is how he treats you compared to Chloe. Are you along for the ride on his trip down memory lane, or …?"

Hope understood exactly what she meant. "I think I was at first. Part of bringing me here was to see if he still felt the same way about me when he was back here, back in the place that he and Chloe shared." She shrugged. "It's not like that, though; it's turned out that this trip has been more about laying her ghost to rest."

"I hope so," said Missy. "I know you're cool about it all, but I hate that he's always said Chloe was the love of his life. I loved her, too, but I want her to let him go."

"She has, but more importantly, he's letting her go, or at least fitting her into a different place in his heart." Hope wondered if she should tell Missy what he'd said about Chloe being his first love and her being the love of his life. She decided against it. Missy was his sister and she was only asking because she cared, but that was private—it was for the two of them to know. If Chance wanted Missy to know, he should tell her himself.

They both turned at the sound of Chance clearing his throat. He stood there leaning in the doorway. His eyes narrowed.

"What?" asked Missy defensively.

He smirked. "I had a feeling you were going to interrogate Hope."

"I'm not interrogating her." She smiled. "Well, only gently. I care, that's all."

"I'm fine."

Missy shook her head at him. "I believe you are, but I care about Hope, too. I wanted to know that she's fine, that you're not hurting her without even knowing it."

Chance frowned and came to stand beside her. "I'm not." He looked down into her eyes. "Am I?"

Hope shook her head. "No. You're not. You're working your way past your grief." Part of her wanted to tell him that the way he was finally coming to terms with his loss didn't hurt her at all, but the way he was taking his time over committing to their future was—just a little bit. She knew she was being impatient, but she wanted him to ask her to marry him.

"Good," said Missy. "That's all I wanted to know, but I promise you both that I'll always stick my nose in where I shouldn't just to make sure that you're both okay."

Chance chuckled. "That's one promise I know you'll keep."

Hope smiled, but talk of promises made her uneasy. Was that why he hadn't asked her to marry him? Saying I do was the most important promise a person could make. Chance didn't make any promises. Ever. How could she expect him to make that one?

Chapter Twelve

It was just after six when they landed back in Bozeman. Chance carried their bags back to his truck and opened the passenger door for Hope. She planted a kiss on his lips before she climbed in.

"Thank you so much for this weekend. I had a great time."

"Thank you for going with me. I had a great time, too. I feel as though we just overcame the only major hurdle we had left. This trip helped me get everything straight in my head."

Hope nodded. "I know. Before we went, I felt like it was taking a risk."

He raised an eyebrow.

"I thought that maybe when you took me there, you'd discover that you couldn't love me."

He shook his head. "I never doubted that I could love you or that I do love you or that I'll love you for the rest of my days. There was no risk there. What I wanted to know was whether I could let go of the past enough to give you the future you deserve."

She smiled. "You're so sweet."

He rolled his eyes and closed the door on her. He went around and climbed into the driver's seat and she laughed. "You really are. You think you hide it so well underneath the badass cowboy exterior, but you're as sweet as Emma."

He chuckled. "No way. I might have a soft center, but I'm nothing like her. She's a smart woman, but she's just a mushy little romantic at heart."

"She is, and Missy was telling me she's a bit of matchmaker, too. I still like her idea of introducing Jack and Dan's mom to my dad. Wouldn't that be awesome if they hit it off."

Chance started up the truck and shook his head at her. "I'd leave it alone, if I were you. I doubt either of them would thank you for it."

"I know." She sighed. "Maybe I'm a bit of a mushy romantic myself." She looked as though something about that bothered her.

"There's nothing wrong with that, is there?"

She shrugged. "I guess not, as long as I don't let it blind me to reality."

"What are you getting at?"

She shrugged again. "I'm just thinking about my dad and wanting him to be happy."

Chance nodded, but he had a feeling that wasn't all she was thinking about. For the first time, he felt like she wasn't telling him the whole truth. He couldn't figure out what might be bothering her, though, and she didn't want to tell him. The safest bet was probably to let it go. She wasn't backward about coming forward and she'd no doubt tell him in her own good time.

When they reached the Davenport ranch, Chance slowed as he drove by Dr. Johnny's house. There was no sign of life. He'd half expected to see them out on the porch or in the yard.

Hope looked around. "Maybe they're out."

He nodded and followed the driveway on toward her dad's place. "Yeah. I'm sure we'll catch up with them soon." He knew she liked to check in with them whenever she could.

Seymour was standing on the front steps when they pulled up. Chance smiled at the way Hope jumped out of the truck and ran up the steps to hug him. He was glad their relationship had improved so much in such a short space of time. Back in Oregon, she'd talked about her father as a cold, distant man whom she didn't really know. Now, she threw herself into his arms like a little girl who'd missed her daddy. That made Chance happy; that was how it should be.

Seymour smiled at him as he trotted up the steps to join them. "Chance. I trust you had a good visit?"

"We did, thanks. My dad sends his regards and says he's looking forward to meeting you."

"I look forward to meeting him, too. Do you have any idea when that might happen?"

Hope answered before Chance could open his mouth. "It won't be for a while yet, not unless you want to take a trip to Summer Lake. Frank's not up to traveling much, is he?" She smiled at Chance, but he sensed a weird tension he didn't understand.

"I think I could be persuaded to tag along, if you two go down there again anytime soon." Seymour smiled. "Don't worry, I wouldn't expect you to hang out with me, but it'd be nice to meet your family, Chance, and I think it's time I paid the Hemmings a visit."

Hope smiled. "I didn't get to meet them, but I did meet their son, Pete. He's a good guy. Chance knows him well, don't you?"

"I do. He's got a good head on his shoulders and he's built a very successful company."

"I thought he'd do well in life. I kept tabs on him for a while." Seymour's smile faded as if he were lost in some thought of his own. He smiled brightly, seeming to remember he wasn't alone. "Maybe I'll give Graham and Anne a call."

"Do it, Dad," said Hope. She looked at Chance and reined in her enthusiasm. "If you think you're ready."

Chance had to smile. She wanted the best for both of them, but she didn't push them. He hoped for Seymour's sake that when he decided he was ready to start exploring the possibilities of living again, he'd discover, just as Chance had himself, that he'd waited so long that he was more than ready.

"What can I get you both? It was kind of you to invite me to dinner, but I thought you'd be tired after your trip. This way I get to see you for a little while and you can still get home with some evening left to enjoy."

"Thanks." Chance appreciated his thoughtfulness. "Plus, this way we get to see you twice. You can come for dinner another night."

"I was thinking that the two of you could come here for dinner."

Hope laughed. "What? Are you going to cook?"

Chance sensed Seymour's discomfort. "No, but the caterers in town would rival any private chef I've had." Seymour looked less confident than Chance had seen him before. "And I was thinking I could try my hand at dessert, so at least one course would be homemade."

Hope's expression softened. There was obviously some significance to that statement that Chance wasn't aware of. "Aww, that'd be lovely, Dad."

Chance smiled as a thought struck him. Seeing Seymour get sentimental seemed to have the same effect on him. "If you're going to make dessert, I'll volunteer to grill." He looked at Hope. "How would you feel about doing the veggies? That way, we could have an entirely homemade meal."

Hope beamed at him. "I love it. Not just homemade, but a family-made meal."

Seymour caught Chance's eye and raised an eyebrow. Was he wondering if Chance had popped the question yet? Chance shook his head slightly. He wanted to ask permission before he did.

At eight-thirty, Seymour looked up at the grandfather clock that stood in the corner of the family room. "Do you need to be getting home?"

Hope laughed. "No, but we'll go if you want rid of us."

Seymour gave her a stern look. "You know better than that, Hopey. I'm thinking of Chance. You've had a long weekend and he has to be back out on the range tomorrow."

Chance nodded. He usually took an extra day off whenever he visited the lake. He needed that extra time when he came back to transition between his lives. He wasn't sure that made any sense, but it felt right to him. At least, it had. This time he was going straight back to work in the morning, but his two worlds didn't seem so separate anymore; Hope was helping him build a bridge between them.

As he walked them down the steps to the truck, Seymour put a hand on Chance's shoulder. "Have you had any more time to look over the ranching contract?"

"I have. I was going to call you about it in the morning." For some reason, it seemed important to him not to discuss the business side of things during family times. "My friend Gabe has gone over it for me." He met Seymour's gaze. "He told me he thinks you must be my biggest fan."

Seymour smiled. "He doesn't need to be smart to see that."

Chance smiled. "Thank you."

"I drew the contract up with Hope in mind, of course. But Hope loves you and that has a huge bearing on how I see you."

Chance nodded and stopped. "Would you come back inside with me a moment?"

Seymour nodded.

Chance threw the keys to Hope. "Could you start the truck up? I'll be right there."

He turned and went back up the steps with Seymour at his side. When they reached the top, Seymour held the door open for him and they stepped inside.

"What is it? Is there a problem?"

Chance shook his head. Now that the moment was here, his heart was pounding in his chest. "No, sir. There's no problem. There's just something I want to ask you."

"What?"

"I ... err. I mean ..." Chance drew in a deep breath to calm himself. He needed to get a grip. He didn't want Seymour to think of him as a mumbling idiot. "Sir, I'd like to ask your permission to marry your daughter."

Seymour smiled and nodded.

When he didn't answer immediately, Chance felt the need to go on. "I know I'm not the kind of guy you'd want her to spend her life with, but I love her. I'm not a rich man, but I'll always take care of her. I promise you I'll do everything in my power to make her happy."

Seymour smiled kindly. "I know you will, son. You must understand that? Do you think I'd have drawn up that contract the way it is if I didn't believe in you, if I didn't believe that the two of you love each other and only want the best for each other?"

"I don't think you would have, no. I'm honored and I'm grateful that you did that, but that's business. This is much more than that. I don't want to be just some business partner who you keep on board to keep Hope safe; I want to be the man you're happy to see your daughter with. I want your blessing, not just your permission."

Seymour grasped his shoulder. "You have it, Chance. You have my blessing and you have my respect. I'm happy you're the one she loves, I'm proud of her that she chose a man of your caliber. Believe me, there aren't many like you."

Chance nodded, he couldn't help smiling. This was what he'd wanted—what he'd needed—to hear. "Thank you."

"What are you two up to?" called Hope.

Seymour grinned. "You'd better get going."

"Yeah, I don't want to keep her waiting."

"Do you know when you'll ask her?"

Chance shook his head. "I'm waiting for inspiration to strike. I want it to be special."

"It will be, no matter what you do."

~ ~ ~

The next morning, after Chance had left for work, Hope took her coffee out onto the back porch. She smiled. This place felt like home now and she was glad to be back. She was going up to see her dad in a little while. Now that she was back in town, and didn't plan to take off again for a while, they were going to get down to work. She couldn't wait. Her cell phone rang and she ran back inside to get it from the kitchen counter. It didn't ring much these days, so she'd gotten out of the habit of carrying it around with her the whole time. She smiled when she saw Gina's name on the display.

"Hi, Gina."

"Hey. How are you? Did you have a good weekend?"

"We did, thanks; it was wonderful."

"Good, I'm glad to hear it. I was a bit worried about you."

"Why?"

Gina laughed. "Because, to all of us, Summer Lake is like this mythical place. We've heard of it, but none of us have ever been there. Chance has always kept his two lives very separate. We're his Montana family, but he has his California family down there. It's always seemed that the two would never meet. You're the first one he's ever allowed to see him in both his lives. I was a little concerned how he'd be with you there."

"I don't think it was as hard for him as he expected. Taking me there was like testing himself, seeing if he could let his two worlds collide."

"So, it went well?"

"Very well. It felt more like his two worlds, Montana and California, but also, past and future were merging and blending, rather than colliding, you know?"

"Damn! That's great. I was worried it might have been a tough time for you, or at least have had some tough moments."

"No, not really. I think he had a few tough moments, but not nearly so much as he'd expected."

"Great, then perhaps someday he'll allow us to meet them. I've heard so much about his sister, Missy, over the years. I'd love to meet her."

"Oh, you'll love her, Gina. She reminds me of you in some ways. She doesn't take any crap, and she speaks her mind."

Gina laughed. "We should get along well, then. What about Renée, did you meet her?"

"I did. I really like her. She was so kind and understanding. She made me feel welcome. Before I went, I was kind of worried that she might see me as an intruder, you know? The woman who was coming in to take her dead sister's place."

"No! That's not what you are, and besides, Chloe's been gone for eighteen years."

"That's what she said. She wants to see Chance happy. They share a bond because of Chloe, but she's more realistic than he is about what that means. I feel close to her, like she's his other sister."

"That's awesome. I can relax now. I kept thinking about you all weekend, hoping you were doing okay."

"Aww, thanks. Gina."

"Hey, it's what friends do, right?"

"I believe so, but I haven't had many friends."

"Well, you do now. You've got four of us here, and it sounds like you made a bunch more in Summer Lake."

Hope smiled. It was true. Thanks to Chance, she now had all these amazing people in her life. He was so much richer than she was in many ways. She might have more money, but he was better off in all the ways that mattered. He had friends, lots of people who cared about him, and he was sharing all that wealth with her. She wished he'd be more relaxed about letting her share her wealth with him. "I did. He keeps saying that I've turned his life around--turned him around—but I feel as though he's done just as much for me."

"That's awesome. You two are perfect for each other. It seems to me that after your trip to the lake, you've got a clear path ahead of you. You just need to get on with your happily ever after now, right?"

"Right," agreed Hope. It really was that simple, wasn't it? Chance would ask her to marry him when he was ready and that would be it; they'd be able to get on with their new life.

"You don't sound convinced. What's wrong?"

"Nothing. Nothing at all. I just hope there's not going to be anything else that comes up to get in our way."

"You'll be fine. Life will always throw something at you, but you've weathered the worst of it. You've already proven that you're strong enough together to overcome the storms."

"Yeah."

"Are you around later this morning?"

"I'm not, no. I'm going up to see my dad to get down to working with him. He gave me a crash course in the basics last week, but today we're going to get down to business."

"Great. I hope you'll have fun."

"I think we will. Sorry, why did you ask?"

"Nothing important. I was just wondering if you wanted to come and ride out with me, if you were free. We can do it another time."

"Oh, I'd love to, let's set something up, can we?" Hope was disappointed to miss out on riding with Gina, but spending time with her dad was more important. "Do you mind if I ask you something?"

"Sure, what's up?"

"Do you think Chance would think I'm crazy if I bought him a horse?"

"Hmm, I don't know about that. Maverick's his special buddy, and he loves all the others as if they were his own."

"I know. I don't just mean any old horse for the sake of buying him one. When we were in Oregon, we went riding one day. He rode a big, gray gelding named Hercules. He had a soft spot for him. He's talked about him a few times since. I asked why he didn't buy him, but he said that Hercules isn't a cow horse and he doesn't get to ride just for fun anymore. I'd like him to ride for fun with me, and I think Hercules would be the perfect horse for him. I think he felt sorry for him because he was stuck there just doing trail rides for tourists, but he used to be a dressage horse."

Gina chuckled. "Hercules sounds perfect for him. Chance learned to ride fast when he came out here; he has a natural bond with the horses. Maybe you should do it. It's easier to get forgiveness than permission, right?"

Hope sighed. "It is, but I was kind of hoping it might be a good idea, a great one even, something that would show him how much I care."

"You don't need to buy him anything to do that."

"I know, it's not about the buying, it's about the horse."

"If you think Chance had a special bond with him, then I say do it."

"Thanks. I think I will."

"Okay. Well, I need to get going if I'm going to take Annie out for an hour before I head up to town. I hope you have a great time with your dad and I'll talk to you soon."

"Okay. Thanks again for asking."

"Bye."

Hope hung up and finished her coffee. She was already loving her life here. Maybe she should set up a regular time to ride with Gina. She'd like that—and Chance didn't seem to have the time very often. She didn't want to depend on him to always be the one to take her. Maybe soon she'd be confident enough to ride out by herself.

Chapter Thirteen

Chance slowed the truck as he approached Dr. Johnny's house. Jean was out in the flower bed by the front door and she looked up and waved.

"Hi, Chance. I hear you're making dinner up at the house tonight."

He nodded, feeling a little guilty. Perhaps they should have invited her and Johnny? "Well, I'm in charge of the grill, Hope's in charge of the veggies, and Seymour's taking care of dessert."

Jean laughed. "That's so wonderful. I never thought I'd see the day Seymour would pitch in to help make dinner."

"It was his suggestion."

Jean nodded. "Yes, he told me as much. I think he was offended when I expressed my surprise, but he can hardly blame me. It's the first time I've known him to do anything like that in forty years."

Chance smiled. He liked Jean; he understood where she was coming from, but he felt the need to defend Seymour. "I think you'll see a lot more changes in him in the coming months. Go easy on him? I think he's ready to start living his life a little differently, and that can be hard. It's easier to stay in your rut than to break out of it."

Jean met his gaze. For a moment, he feared he'd offended her, but she nodded slowly and smiled. "Thank you, Chance. I hadn't thought about it like that, but you're right. He's trying to open up, isn't he? He's experimenting with letting himself really live again. He needs our support, not teasing."

Chance smiled, glad she understood.

"You're a smart one, aren't you?"

He shrugged. "I don't know about that, but I can relate to where he's coming from."

"I'll bet you can, but you're a few steps ahead of him, aren't you?"

"Yeah. I guess I am."

"Do you think we might be hearing the sound of wedding bells any time soon?"

He frowned.

"I'm sorry. That's overstepping. It's none of my business."

"No, it's not that. I don't mind you asking. I just … I guess …" He didn't know how to explain it, so he decided to just spit it out and say it. "I want to marry her. I want to ask her. I've asked for and received Seymour's blessing. What I don't know is the best way to ask Hope. I keep thinking I want to make some big gesture, but I don't know what she might like."

Jean smiled kindly. "She likes you. She loves you. You should do what comes naturally to you, Chance. Hope isn't the kind of girl who needs fireworks and grand gestures. She just needs to know that you love her. That she's the most important thing in the world to you."

Chance nodded. He'd heard it before and he knew the truth of it, but it didn't help him figure out what to do. "No big ideas, then?" he asked with a rueful smile.

Jean shook her head. "Sorry, you're on your own with that one. I'd better let you get going, too; I don't want to be the reason you're late for dinner, especially since they're counting on you for the main course."

"Yeah, I'd better get up there. If we don't poison ourselves, maybe we can do it again soon and invite you and Dr. Johnny."

"That'd be nice, but it's important for the three of you to bond first, build a good foundation as a family."

"Yeah." He tipped his hat to her and pointed his truck up the driveway to Seymour's place. When he pulled up in front of the house, he sat there for a moment. He didn't like to just run up the steps and let himself in. He wasn't comfortable enough to do that yet. On the other hand, he hated the thought of ringing the doorbell and waiting to be let in like a visitor. He fished his phone out of his pocket and called Hope.

"Hey, are you going to be here soon? Dad and I got a great day's work done, but we should start thinking about dinner soon."

"I just pulled up."

"Great."

He looked up to see the front door open and she came outside and smiled at him. "Are you coming up?" she asked with a smile.

"On my way." He hung up and grabbed the cooler off the backseat.

She greeted him with a kiss at the top of the stairs. "How was your day?"

He nodded. "It was good, business as usual, but I'm worried about Maverick. He's favoring his offside hind leg again. He's not lame, but he's feeling it. I want to rest him up tomorrow, but I don't know who I'll take out instead. Rio's gone on the guest ranch roster now, so he's not available."

She smiled. "It sounds to me like you need another horse or two to call your own. What about Archie? Did you talk to Lily about him?"

"I did; in fact, I called her today about him." He shook his head. "It's probably a bad idea."

"Why's that?"

"Because he's not the ideal candidate. I'd have to train him to be a cow horse. He's young and headstrong, and there are probably a dozen more suitable horses right here in the valley that I could buy and not have to transport here from California."

"How do you go about transporting horses over long distances like that? Is it hard for them, do they hate it?"

Chance shrugged. "It depends on the animal. Some of them travel well, some of them don't. It's not ideal for them, but it's a fact of life."

Hope nodded, looking thoughtful.

"I'll figure something out." He held up the cooler. "For now, I'm more interested in getting to work on dinner. These ribeyes should be pretty good."

He followed her through to the kitchen where the sight of Seymour wearing an apron and with a smudge of flour on his cheek made Chance smile. The guy looked so much less intimidating like that. In fact, he looked kind of vulnerable, and, for the first time, Chance noticed how old he looked.

"Don't laugh," he said with a rueful smile. "I'm new to this baking lark and I haven't mastered it yet."

"I have no doubt you will, though," said Chance with a smile.

"The results have been wonderful so far," said Hope.

Chance nodded his agreement. Hope had brought home a batch of Seymour's cookies earlier in the week and they were good. Very good.

Seymour nodded at the cooler. "What are we having?"

"Rib-eyes."

"Perfect. I'll pick us out a decent red, then."

Chance hesitated. He didn't want to decline whatever wine Seymour might offer, but he did want to offer an alternative. He reached into the holdall he'd slung over his shoulder and pulled out a bottle of the Cab Franc. "I know it's not what you're used to, but would you at least give this a try?"

Hope looked a little surprised, but Seymour nodded eagerly. "I'd love to. I've been stuck in a rut with my wines, I need the encouragement to try something new."

Chance smiled, remembering his conversation with Jean not ten minutes ago. "You might not like it, and we can crack open one of yours, if that's the case, but you might find you love it. And if you do, I've got a couple of bottles in here, and I'll get you a case sent over."

"Thanks."

~ ~ ~

Hope smiled to herself. She loved the dynamic between the two men. They were both tough guys who, for probably the first time in their lives, were allowing themselves to be vulnerable—and to help each other out. She loved them both for it and she loved that she was the one who had brought them together, and more than that, brought them to the point in their lives where they each were right now.

"Shall I get some glasses?" she asked.

"Please," said her dad, holding up his floury hands. "I probably shouldn't do it."

She brought the glasses and Chance poured Seymour a taste. She was proud of them both—that Chance didn't pour a full glass to start with and that her dad didn't make a big deal of swilling and sniffing. He took a sip and smiled. "This is good."

"Really?" asked Chance. "You don't have to drink it just to be polite."

Hope laughed. "Believe me, he wouldn't. I can tell by his face that he likes it."

"I like it a lot," said her dad with a grin.

Chance raised an eyebrow at Hope. "Is a lot code for, I can stand a glass or two of this stuff?"

She laughed again. "It's more likely code for, I like it so much I might buy the winery."

They both laughed with her. "I hadn't thought of that," said her dad, "but now you mention it …"

"I don't think the guys who own the place would ever sell out, but I think they'd probably love it if you want to invest."

"You know them?"

"Kind of," Chance said with a smile.

For the next half hour, they all worked with and around each other in the kitchen. Chance prepared the steaks. Hope was a little concerned that they might be too plain for her dad's taste. All Chance did was salt and pepper them on each side and then he left them to sit while he got the grill ready. Her dad kept himself busy at the island, preparing sheets of cookies and little cakes. She wasn't sure what the cakes might be; they were a new one on her, but it didn't matter. He was enjoying himself doing something simple and spending time with her and Chance. She prepared a big salad and sautéed a huge pan of green beans. They were one thing she knew both her dad and Chance loved. It was hardly the healthy option, but she cooked them in butter with mushrooms and garlic and a good splash of the wine.

Once her dad had taken his last tray of cookies from the oven, he smiled at her. "Do you mind if I go and talk to Chance while he grills?"

She raised an eyebrow, wondering what he might want to talk to him about.

He smiled. "Stop worrying. I'm not going to interrogate him. I want to learn from him. I haven't grilled a steak since we lived here. I've forgotten how, and I wasn't very good at it then. I want to learn again, and I have a feeling your Chance is the man to teach me."

She smiled. "He does grill a great steak and burgers and kebabs and pretty much anything on the grill."

"See?" He came and dropped a kiss on the top of her head. "He can teach me a lot."

She smiled to herself as she watched him go. Things were working out so well—for him as well as for her.

Once the beans were almost ready, she left them on a low light and made a light salad dressing; she didn't want anything to detract from the steak. Once she was done, she looked around the kitchen, and finding nothing left to do, she went to check on Chance and her dad. She slowed when she saw them out on the deck and her throat tightened. She didn't know what she'd done to deserve two such amazing men in her life. They were polar opposites in some respects and yet so similar in others.

Chance was turning the steaks and her dad was watching closely, asking questions all the time. She moved closer, enjoying seeing them getting along so well. It seemed they weren't talking about the steaks, but about the ranch.

"I expect you to run the herd however you see fit, and I have every faith that will be the right way. I'm not doubting you, Chance."

"I know." Watching his face, Hope knew Chance was frustrated. He was trying to make a point but hadn't chosen the right words to get it across. "What I mean is …" He shrugged. "I promise you, I won't let you down."

Hope's jaw dropped. Had she heard that right? Had Chance just made a promise?

Her dad turned and saw her. "Are you coming out to join us?"

She shook her head. "I just wanted to see how long the steaks will be. Everything else is ready to go."

Chance met her gaze with a smile. "Two minutes. Then we can let them sit a minute or two while we dish up." He looked at Seymour. "You always need to let the steaks sit and keep cooking a minute or two when you take them off the grill, it helps the flavor to no end. And don't ever do that fancy eat your salad first thing. You dish the salad right up along with everything else. The meat is the star of this show."

Her dad smiled. "See, Hopey. I told you I had a lot to learn."

She nodded and went back through to the kitchen. She was still trying to process hearing Chance make a promise. He didn't do that. Ever. What had changed?

~ ~ ~

It was dark by the time they left Seymour's place. Chance looked at Hope as he pulled away from the house. "Are you okay?" It had been a great evening, but she'd been quieter than usual while they ate.

"I'm a little tired. That's all."

He nodded. She had been working with her dad all day before he arrived. "We'd best get you home to bed, then."

"Yeah, that sounds good."

That wasn't the response he'd been hoping for, but maybe she was too tired to joke around with him. And he shouldn't be thinking about what they could do in bed other than sleep. He reached over and touched her arm. "You really are beat, aren't you?"

She met his gaze and shook her head. "No, I'm not that tired at all, if I'm honest. And I need to be honest."

"Why, what's up?" Something was bothering her, and it looked like something big.

"When you were grilling the steaks with Dad, I heard you make him a promise."

Chance wondered what she was getting at. "I did. I promised him I won't let him down, and I won't. I'm a man of my word."

"I know that. You've always been a man of your word, but I thought you were a man who didn't make promises. Ever."

He nodded slowly. "Yeah. I haven't made a promise for eighteen years, as you know."

"So, what changed?"

He shrugged. "When we were at the lake and I saw Renée, we talked about that. I told you that being there made me see that so many of the things I believed about life and about myself were just old superstitions that I clung to in an attempt to still feel close to Chloe. Renée kicked my butt about the promises thing. She pointed out that the promise I made to her that night probably didn't make any difference to what happened, and, that even if it had, it was time to forget it, to let it go like everything else."

Hope nodded.

"What's the matter? I thought you might be pleased. I can see how dumb it was now, but it was important to me for all those years."

She smiled, but it didn't reach her eyes. "I am pleased. That's a huge step for you."

Chance turned off East River Road into the driveway of Remington Ranch. "You don't sound pleased."

When he pulled up in front of the cabin, she reached across and hugged him. "I am. I'm happy for you. I'm being silly, that's all."

"Want to tell me about it?"

She shook her head. "If you don't mind, I'd rather let it go. I know I'm being stupid, so let me talk myself around?"

"Okay." He didn't like to see her upset and not understand why. He didn't like that she didn't want to explain it to him, but if anyone could understand, it was him. That had been his MO all these years. He didn't explain himself. He went off by himself and worked through whatever was bothering him and came back when he felt better about it. He was trying not to do that with Hope. They were a team; they said they'd tell each other everything.

She opened the truck door and got out. "Come on, it's late."

He got out and slid his arm around her shoulders on their way into the cabin. "Whatever it is, don't let it blow up in your mind?"

She reached up and planted a kiss on his cheek. "That's what I'm talking myself out of. I don't want you to see how silly I was being. I just need to talk myself down."

"I won't think you're silly."

She smiled, and it was more genuine this time. "I know."

Chapter Fourteen

On Saturday morning, Hope greeted Chance with a smile when he came into the kitchen, and handed him a mug of coffee. "There you go, sleepyhead."

He took it and planted a peck on her lips. "Thanks, honey. You're up early."

"I couldn't sleep."

"Is everything okay?"

"Yeah, I'm fine. I've always loved to watch the sunrise. I think this is the most beautiful place in the world to watch it. All the stars slowly fade as the sky gets lighter, then comes the glow and then finally, the sun comes up and ushers in the new day and a whole new beginning. I love it." She shook her head. "Sorry, just listen to me. I think there is a mushy romantic hiding in my head somewhere and she comes out to play now and then."

Chance smiled. "Don't apologize; I like the way you describe it. I've never thought of the sunrise as a new beginning before, but it really is, isn't it?"

"Yeah, I don't think I'd thought of it like that before, either. I was just rambling and it came out. My mind is all over the place because it's been working overtime on everything Dad's been teaching me this week. I want to get started, but he doesn't want me to yet. He wants me to practice for a while first."

Chance raised an eyebrow. "How do you do that? I thought you either bought and sold shares or you didn't. How do you practice?"

She smiled. "When you're practicing, you just pretend. You don't actually buy stocks, you just keep note of what you would have bought and sold each day and keep track of what your outcome would have been if you had."

"That makes sense. You don't risk anything till you know what you're doing."

"Exactly, but you don't make anything, either. Yesterday, I had a really great day, on paper. If I'd bought instead of just pretending to, I would have made a very nice profit at the end of the day."

"He just wants you to be careful, right? He wants you to get the hang of what you're doing before you put any money on the line."

"I know; I'm impatient, that's all."

He smiled. "You'll get there."

"I will, but in the meantime, my brain is constantly buzzing with it. I've spent an hour on my laptop already this morning, going through it all."

"That's good. You wanted to find something you could really get involved with. It sounds like this could be it."

"I think it is. I'm loving everything about it, not just the working with my dad. And how about you? How did you sleep?"

"Very well. I was dead to the world until just now. I hate that I have to work most of the day, though. What are you going to do?"

"Don't worry about me. I think I'm going to sit here and work."

"You should go out and have some fun. See what the girls are up to or go see your dad or something." He didn't like the thought of her sitting here cooped up with her computer all day.

Her smile put his mind at ease. "That's what I'm saying; this is fun. I'm going to go sit out back with my laptop and have the best of both worlds. I'll have the fresh air and mountains all around me and the world of finance at my fingertips."

Chance chuckled. "I reckon your dad is going to have to start calling you mini-me soon."

She pushed his shoulder. "No, he won't. I'm not aiming for world domination, just to carve out a nice little niche for myself. I need to feel useful."

"You are useful. You're amazing and I love you."

"I love you, too."

"How about I take you out for dinner tonight?"

Her eyes widened; he knew she liked the idea. "You don't have to do that."

"I know, but I want to." He couldn't tell her that he was planning on asking her to marry him. He still hadn't come up with any big ideas about how to ask her, so he'd finally accepted that he'd just have to be himself. They could go out for a nice dinner. He'd been thinking he'd ask her there; or maybe when they came home, he could ask her out on the back porch. It was a place she loved to be and it'd be underneath the big starry Montana sky she loved so much. That was about as special as he could think of. "We could go to the Yellowstone Valley Lodge."

She made a face. "Or we could go to Chico. The restaurant is just as good, and I know you feel more at home there."

He smiled. "I do, but stepping out of my comfort zone isn't a bad thing." He was finding that it was a very good thing. Asking her to marry him was stepping out of his comfort zone, but he knew if she said yes, it'd be the best move he'd ever made.

"It isn't, but I like Chico, too. To tell you the truth, I feel more comfortable there."

"Chico it is, then." He wasn't going to argue, if that was where she wanted to go.

"What time do you think you'll be back?"

"Early. I'm hoping to be able to get back by four-thirty, five at the latest."

"Okay. I'll make sure I'm finished up by then."

He chuckled. "I'll see you later."

He went to her and hugged her to him. She slid her arms around his waist and rested her head against his chest, making him smile. His heart raced in his chest at the thought that, hopefully, this time tomorrow, she'd be his fiancée—and soon, she'd be his wife.

~ ~ ~

Hope checked herself over in the mirror. She looked good, even if she did say so herself. She'd taken the first shower so she could finish getting ready while Chance took his. She was already used to sharing a bathroom with him. She smiled, remembering how she'd never allowed Drew into her dressing room or bathroom. He had his own. The master suite in her house had his and her closets and bathrooms. She couldn't see Chance ever wanting to spend much time there, but she knew that when they did visit, she'd want them to share her bathroom, not be separate.

Chance poked his head around the bedroom door. "Are you nearly ... wow!"

She turned around to face him with a smile.

"You look amazing."

"Thank you." It was hard to strike the right balance out here. Everyone wore jeans pretty much all the time. Getting dressed up meant nice jeans and a nicer top than usual. She'd managed to find the perfect combination when she was back in LA—a pair of butt-hugging skinny jeans and a silver gray top with flowing sleeves and cutout shoulders. "I'm glad you like it."

"I love it. There's only one problem with it." His eyes narrowed and he rubbed his chin as if he were trying to come up with a solution to that problem.

"What's that?"

"It makes me want to stay here instead of going out. It looks so good on you, that all I can think of is getting you out of it." He came into the bedroom wearing just a towel around his waist. His muscular chest was still glistening from the shower.

She laughed. "It'd be easier for me to get you out of that." She reached out and grabbed the edge of the towel and tugged.

Chance laughed and tugged back. "No!"

"Aww, but you look so good. I want to get you out of what you're wearing, too."

He clung to the towel and shook his head, backing away to the corner of the room as she followed him.

"Give me the towel."

He shook his head. "No, seriously. If you take my towel, then we won't be going anywhere other than bed this evening."

She laughed. "And that's a problem?"

It seemed it was. His expression clouded over and she could tell he was going through an internal struggle. It wasn't like him to turn her down.

He shrugged. "You know I want to, but I want us to go out, too. I want to take you to a nice place for a nice dinner and feel like I'm giving you what you deserve."

She waggled her eyebrows at him. "I think you could give me what I deserve right here in bed."

He shook his head at her. "But if we go out now, then you can still have your way with me when we get home. If you have your way with me first, we won't feel up to going out."

"We might." She knew he was right, but she didn't want to wait.

He shook his head again with a wicked grin. "Nah. By the time I'm done with you, you'll be too tired to go anywhere."

"Ooh, I like the sound of that."

"So do I; so, let's hurry up and go out so that we can hurry up and get back."

"Okay," she said with a sigh. "But it's you who needs to hurry up. I'm about ready. I'll be out on the porch waiting for you."

He kissed her as she made her way out of the bedroom and she made another grab for the towel. He dodged neatly out of the way with a smile. "Patience!"

She laughed. "Not one of my virtues, I'm afraid."

"Yeah, mine either. I'll be down in a few."

When they got to Chico, the parking lot was crowded. They had to drive around for a while to find a space. Hope chuckled. "It amazes me that there's nothing around here, just a couple of houses and nothing else for miles, but yet the parking lot is full."

Chance nodded. "It's like this all through the summer, and most weekends in the winter, too."

"We could always go back home, or …" she raised an eyebrow at him. "I seem to remember you mentioning the back of your truck one time. We could go for a drive and …" she waggled her eyebrows at him, "get in the back of your truck and … stargaze."

His eyes twinkled and she could tell he liked the idea, but he shook his head. "No, we came for dinner."

She pouted. "We might not even get a table if it's this busy."

"We've got a table. I called ahead."

"On this short notice? We only talked about it this morning."

He shrugged. "I know people."

She had to laugh at the way he said it.

"What?" he asked with a chuckle. "This might not be your fancy LA nightlife, but it still helps to know people around here."

"I'm suitably impressed."

"Yeah, right."

"I am!" She laughed as he held the door open for her and bid her to enter with a bow and a flourish of his arm.

The dining room, as they called the restaurant here, hadn't changed since she was a kid. She remembered coming here with her parents and her aunt and uncle and all her cousins. For a moment, she was swept back in time.

"Are you okay?" Chance put a hand on her shoulder.

"I'm fine, sorry. I just got hit with a whole load of memories. This place hasn't changed a bit." She felt as though she had some understanding of how difficult their visit to Summer Lake must have been for him.

"Do you want to leave?"

"No. It's nothing bad, it just took me by surprise, took my breath away." She smiled. "I miss my mom, but it's kind of comforting to come back to places that I came to with her."

Chance nodded and placed a hand in the small of her back to guide her through the crowd to the host station. The guy at the desk looked up and grinned when he saw Chance. "Hey! I thought it must be a joke when they told me to keep a table for you." He looked at Hope and smiled. "Now, I get it."

Chance smiled. "Hope, I'd like you to meet Steve. Steve, this is …"

"Hope Davenport," Steve finished for him. "It's a pleasure to meet you. I met your cousins a couple of months ago, but I didn't think you came up here anymore." He smiled at Chance. "But I hope we'll be seeing more of you now."

Hope nodded, but was a little put out. "You saw my cousins?"

"Yes, TJ and Reid were in a couple of months back."

"Wow. I didn't know they'd been up here." She smiled. "Sorry, you took me by surprise mentioning them. It's lovely to meet you, Steve, and you'd better get used to me. I just moved back here."

Steve's eyes widened in surprise. "Wow. Then welcome home!" He smiled at Chance. "That's wonderful news."

Chance nodded, and Hope got the impression that he didn't want the conversation to move on to why she'd come back or where she was living.

"It is," she said. "And I'm looking forward to finding out if the food here is as good as I remember."

"I think you'll find it's even better. Let me show you to your table." He led them through the restaurant to a quieter area in the back. This was a smaller room with fewer tables and a more elegant feel than the main dining room. Steve took them to a table by the fireplace with a wonderful view of Emigrant Peak through the picture window. "Best table in the house," he said. "Nothing but the best for my friend here." He smiled at Chance, who punched his arm. "Thanks. I owe you one."

"He seems nice," said Hope when Steve had gone. "Is he a good friend of yours?"

"Yeah, I guess you could call him that. He helps with the herd when I need him. He works here and he's with the Fire Department, too. He's a good guy."

"Do you have many friends?" It occurred to her that she didn't know about his friends here. She'd met a whole gang of them in Summer Lake, but Steve was the first one she'd even heard mention of here in the valley.

He shrugged. "I have the guys. I have four honorary brothers who are also my best friends. And I know some people, too." He smiled. "Guys aren't like girls when it comes to friends. We see each other when we see each other. We don't need to make time for each other in the way girls seem to."

Hope shrugged. "I wouldn't know about that. I don't really have any friends at all. The only one I had in LA was Toby; the rest were just acquaintances, contacts."

"Aww." He reached across the table and patted her hand. "You do now. You have four friends here who'll soon be your family."

Hope's heart jumped into her throat, then she took a deep calming breath. That was silly. He didn't necessarily mean they'd be her sisters-in-law. He could just mean they would be her honorary family just as all the brothers were his.

He didn't notice her reaction and continued, "And you've got Miss and Emma and all the others at the lake."

She nodded. "I can see me and Renée becoming good friends if we do spend any time there."

The waiter came with their menus and recited the specials to them. Chance ordered a bottle of wine, and Hope was glad they'd come here; she loved seeing him relaxed and at ease in his environment.

When the waiter had gone, he asked, "Wouldn't that be weird for you?"

"Wouldn't what be weird?"

"You were saying you could see you and Renée becoming good friends …"

She smiled. "It wouldn't be weird for me at all. I like her. I want to get to know her better." Her smile faded. "Or would that be too weird for you?"

"No!" He reached across the table and took hold of her hand again. "That'd be awesome, not weird."

"Good, because I like her a lot. I want to know more about her women's center."

Chance frowned. "Why?"

"Because, I make some pretty big charitable donations every year." She frowned back at him. "I'm not talking charity, so don't look at me like that."

He raised an eyebrow at her and smirked.

"Oh, you! I am talking about her charity, but you know what I mean. The donations I make are tax write-offs for me. They help me. I try to make sure that I get involved with causes I believe in, that the money is going to people who really need it, people for whom it will make a difference. The women's center seems like a great cause. I believe Renée would put the money to good use and she can certainly make a difference in people's lives with what she's doing there. Don't you think?"

He shrugged.

"What, you disagree?"

"I don't know. I don't really even know what a women's center does."

She had to smile. "You're such a guy."

He laughed and looked down at his lap. "Yup, last time I checked, I still had a pair."

She laughed and shook her head at him. "You're so bad!"

He gave her a sexy smile. "Isn't that what you love about me?"

She nodded. "It is. I love that you're so bad and so good all at once."

"Especially in bed?" He hooked his foot around her calf and rubbed it up and down.

She felt the heat in her cheeks as the waiter came back to take their order.

Once they'd ordered, and he'd gone, she narrowed her eyes at Chance. "You were the one who wouldn't let me keep you home in bed, and now you're tormenting me out in public."

He smirked. "I've got to make sure you'll still want me by the time we get home."

"You've got no worries there." She couldn't wait!

The evening flew by as they talked and laughed. Hope loved every minute of it. Chance was quite the charmer when he was relaxed and enjoying himself, and he certainly seemed to be both of those tonight. He was flirting with her in a way he hadn't before and she loved it. Part of her didn't want the evening to end, but another part was still eager to get him home. She couldn't wait to see what this new, playful side of him would want to get up to in bed.

After their plates were cleared and the wine was gone, the waiter returned to see if they wanted anything else.

Chance raised an eyebrow and she shook her head. She did want something, but she wasn't going to get it here.

Chance asked for the bill and his mood seemed to change.

"Is everything all right?"

"Yeah. It's all good, honey. I've had a great time. Have you?"

"Wonderful, and the evening isn't over yet."

He was fidgeting with something in his pocket and didn't meet her gaze. "You're right. It isn't." He looked up and smiled at her, then reached across the table and took hold of her hand. "There's something I'd like to ask you before we go. I've been wanting to ask you all night. I didn't want to mess it up and now I think I've left it too late."

"What is it?"

He sucked in a deep breath and smiled. "Honey, I want to ask you if—"

They both jumped as a flash of light illuminated their table. Chance jumped to his feet, but Hope sat tight and put her head down. She knew what it was.

Chapter Fifteen

"Hope! Hope," called a voice. She couldn't see its owner, or much of anything else, blinded as she still was by the camera flash. "What are you doing here? Are you here visiting with your father?" He turned to Chance. "Are the two of you back together? Did she leave Matt to get back with you?"

"Chance!" she cautioned him. He looked like he was about to punch the guy. "Don't." Her tone was enough to make him pause and look at her. It was a plea, not a command. "Please?"

Steve appeared behind the guy and put an arm around his neck. He dragged him away before he could ask any more questions or raise his camera again. When they'd gone, Hope closed her eyes and blew out a big sigh. That was the worst end to the most perfect evening.

Chance sat back down heavily in his chair. His jaw was clenched and his fists were balled tight. Hope was grateful that Steve had appeared when he did. She hated to think what Chance might have done otherwise.

"I'm sorry," she murmured.

"It's not your fault." He ground the words out through clenched teeth.

She reached for his hand, but his fists were still clenched. She stroked his wrist until he started to relax a little. The wild look left his eyes and he seemed to come back to her. He met her gaze. "I'm sorry."

"You did nothing wrong. You did well to hold back when he pounced on us like that."

"You have no idea."

Unfortunately, Hope felt like she did have some idea, and she didn't like it.

Steve came hurrying back to the table. "I'm so sorry. Your dinner is on the house, of course. I've got him in the cold store. I'll keep him there till you're gone or call in the police—whatever you prefer we do with him."

Chance shook his head. "I know what I'd like to do with him."

Hope sighed. "I think it'd be best if we leave and you let him go once we're out of here." She met Steve's gaze. "I don't want you getting in trouble on my account."

"I won't be in any kind of trouble. We don't stand for that kind of thing around here."

Hope nodded. She had a feeling Chance wouldn't be alone in his reaction to such an invasion of privacy. If the press was going to find its way here to Montana, they'd need to be careful.

"Do you want me to bring your truck around?" Steve pointed to an emergency exit just beyond the fireplace.

To her surprise, Chance nodded and handed over his keys.

They sat in silence for a few moments until they saw headlights flashing outside. They got up and went out. The truck was on the grass right outside the door.

Steve grasped Chance's shoulder. "I'm sorry, bud."

Hope was relieved to see the tension around Chance's eyes ease a little. "It's not your fault. Thanks for taking care of it."

Steve nodded grimly. "You don't need any trouble. You remember that if he shows up again."

Chance nodded and opened the passenger door for Hope to get in. "Come on, honey; let's go home."

They drove back in silence. Hope felt as though the little bubble she'd been living in had burst. The press had left her alone since she'd been here and she'd started to believe that it would be permanent. How likely were they to come all the way up here? But they had. Or at least that one guy had.

Chance looked across at her as he drove down East River Road. "Are you okay?"

"Yeah. I'm just sad. I thought the press might leave me alone. I should have known better."

He nodded.

"How are you?"

He blew out a sigh. "Calming down a little. I wanted to " He stopped himself and fixed his gaze back on the road ahead.

She touched his arm. "So did I, but it wouldn't do any good. It'd only make things worse. Maybe he was just an opportunist. He might be a freelancer who's here on vacation and just happened to spot us."

Chance pursed his lips. "That'd be a hell of a coincidence."

"I know, but it helps me to think that way."

"If it helps, then you think it, but I've got a nasty feeling he's just the first of many."

She nodded her agreement. "Even if he is, it'll blow over. We'll be news for a little while and then they'll move on. The media doesn't have a very long attention span."

"I guess."

"Listen, we were having a great time until he showed up. We can't let him spoil our evening."

"He already did." He said it with such finality that she almost shut up and let him brood, but she didn't want their wonderful evening to end that way.

"He didn't, though, not if we don't let him. We can just pick up right where we were. You were about to ask me something."

Chance turned off the road and drove the length of the driveway to the ranch with lips pressed together in a thin line.

"I was."

"So why don't you ask me now?"

He shot a quick look at her and shook his head. "Nope."

When he pulled up in front of the cabin, he got out of the truck and waited for her. She didn't follow. She sat there and waited for him to come around to her. He opened the door and she smiled in the face of his irritation.

"What's up?"

"Nothing. I just thought I'd sit here and wait to see if a sexy cowboy happens along. You never know. If one does, he might pick me up and carry me away to his bed."

He pursed his lips, but she could see there was the hint of a smile lurking at the corners of his mouth.

"You don't think I'm in luck?"

He shook his head. "The only cowboy around here is mighty pissed off right now."

"That's a shame. If there were a cowboy with an open mind around who wanted to carry me to his bed, I'd make it worth his while." She waited. This time there was more than the hint of a smile.

"How?" he asked eventually.

She smirked. "Oh, he'd have to take me there to find that out. I don't like to spoil surprises."

He blew out a sigh. "I'm not in the mood for games."

"That's the best time to play them; they cheer you up and take your mind off your troubles. And I think you'll like the game I have in mind."

He finally smiled and wrapped one arm around her shoulders and slid the other under her legs. She wrapped her arms around his neck and hung on tight as he carried her out of the truck and into the cabin. He carried her through to the bedroom and went back to lock the front door—something she'd never known him do before.

She struck a sexy pose when he came back in, but he shook his head. "I love you, honey; thank you for making me smile again, but I am so not in the mood."

She reached her arms up to him and he lay down on the bed beside her. They held each other close in a way that was all about caring and closeness and nothing about sex. She stroked his hair and planted a kiss on his cheek. "I'm not in the mood any more, either; I just wanted to see you smile again."

He pulled back and planted a peck on her lips. "How do you do it? How do you manage to find the bright side so quickly? How do you let go of all the anger and choose to smile instead? I know your way is better than mine, but I have no idea how the hell you do it."

She shrugged. "It's a choice. I learned a long time ago that we don't get to choose what happens to us. All we can choose is how we react to it, how we deal with it. I choose to find the bright side because it makes me feel better. I don't like to feel angry, I don't like to feel hopeless." She shrugged. "You and I both know that sometimes life really is too short. I don't want to waste any of it feeling bad."

Chance hugged her to him. "I want to be more like that."

"It's a choice, it really is."

He nodded. "I'm starting to understand that, thanks to you."

~ ~ ~

They lay that way for a long time, holding each other close. Chance knew the moment she fell asleep. She gave a little sigh and he felt her body relax against him. He was glad she could drift off. He doubted he'd be getting any sleep tonight.

He blew out a sigh. The evening had been going so well; they'd had such a great time. Okay, so maybe he'd blown a couple of chances to ask her to marry him. He'd kept thinking he'd do it in a minute. Then dinner had been over. They were ready to leave, but he'd wanted to ask her before they did. Just when he'd been about to, that asshole with the camera had ruined everything. He unclenched his fist. He was proud of himself. He hadn't let his instincts take over. He hadn't floored the guy. He couldn't take all the credit for that; he'd been about to when Hope had stopped him. She'd only said one word—Don't. That was all it had taken for him to stop. His anger hadn't magically disappeared, but it had receded enough for sense to prevail. Then Steve had appeared and dragged the guy away.

Wasn't it just his luck that at the very moment he'd been about to ask Hope to marry him, a damned photographer had appeared out of nowhere? It was bad enough that they invaded her privacy at all, but this one had managed to spoil the most important moment of his life.

Hope stirred and smiled sleepily at him. "Are you okay?"

"I'm fine, honey. Go back to sleep."

Her eyes closed and she was gone again. He wasn't sure she'd even been fully awake. He had to smile. It seemed that, even in her sleep, she could sense his anger and calm him down. She was good for him. He sighed. He wanted to be good for her. He didn't want to be the guy who was always pissed off about something. He didn't want to dampen her bright spirit. He thought back to her words before she'd gone to sleep. It's a choice. She truly believed that. He'd never felt like it was a choice. He didn't choose to get angry, he didn't choose to dwell on the pain and the negatives. At least, he'd never thought he did. They were just natural reactions to things that happened. But, as Hope had said, even though you couldn't choose what happened, you could choose how you reacted. His anger wasn't necessarily a natural reaction, it was just an automatic one. If it was a conscious choice, then he wouldn't react the way he did. He'd much rather choose the same path that Hope chose. He'd rather find the bright side and let things go. He nodded to himself as he lay there. He was going to try it. He knew it wouldn't be easy, but if he could learn to do it, it would be well worth it.

He lay there a while longer thinking about how he could start making different choices. He hadn't thought he'd be able to sleep at all, but as he considered the options for finding a bright side to what had happened this evening, he started to get drowsy. He turned on his shoulder and rested his arm across Hope's waist. He'd hit on an idea—an idea that helped everything. He was going to ask her to marry him, and he knew she'd love it. He also knew that it'd be taking her advice and putting it into practice. It'd mean waking up early, though. He closed his eyes and smiled. He had no doubt that he'd be awake when he needed to be.

It was still dark when he opened his eyes again. He turned over to check the clock on the nightstand. Yep. He'd made it. There was still an hour before sunrise. He almost got out of bed to go and put the coffee on, but he hesitated and kissed Hope on the forehead before he did. That was a new superstition he'd hooked onto, but it was a good one. After the way he'd left her in Oregon, he didn't like to get out of bed without letting her know where he was going.

"Hmm?" she muttered sleepily.

"Honey, I want you to think about waking up. I'm going to put the coffee on."

"Hmm? Why? It's not light yet."

"I know, but I have a surprise for you. Trust me?"

"Mmm. You know I do. With my life, but I might need some of that coffee before I can unglue my eyelids."

He smiled. "You snooze on for a few minutes; I'll be back."

While the coffee brewed, he ran outside to his truck with some supplies. He wanted this to be perfect. He stuffed everything into the box in the pickup bed and stepped back. Was he forgetting anything? Damn! Just the most important thing. He ran back inside to get it. Then poured two mugs of coffee. He smiled when he heard Hope in the bathroom, glad that she was up of her own accord.

She smiled at him blearily when she came into the kitchen. "What are we doing, Chancey bear? It's Sunday morning. I thought I might get to keep you in bed for a while."

He handed her the coffee mug and planted a kiss on her lips. "Trust me, this is going to be even better than that."

She gave him a doubtful look. "Nothing is better than getting to stay in bed with you—on Sunday morning or any other time."

He chuckled. "Thank you, but I'll ask you if you still feel that way when we get back."

She raised an eyebrow at him over the rim of her mug. "Okay, then. I'd better drink this and work on being awake. It'll have to be something very special indeed to make me change my mind."

He took her mug away from her again and laughed at the horrified look she gave him. "Don't worry. I'm just putting it in here so you can bring it with you." He poured it into a travel mug and did the same with his own. "There. Now we can go."

"I don't get to take a shower or get dressed?"

He shook his head. "No time and no need. And besides, you look cute." She did, too. He loved the pajamas she wore around the cabin in the mornings. They were simple cotton things, but they clung to her breasts and her gorgeous rounded ass.

He took her by the arm and turned her around to march her out the door.

"Don't I even need a jacket or anything?"

"Nope. I've got a couple in the truck if you get cold."

"Okay, then, here we go." She gave him a happy little smile and went out to the truck.

He loved that she was so willing to go along with him. There were no questions, no reluctance at all.

He kept his eyes peeled for deer as he drove down East River Road. They were always active in the early morning. When they were a few miles south of the ranch, he took a left onto Bridger Lane.

"Are you going to tell me where we're going?" asked Hope. She was looking more awake as the truck bumped along the rutted dirt road.

"Nope." He smiled at her. "I don't want to spoil the surprise."

"Okay, then. I guess I'll just sit here and drink my coffee."

It took about fifteen minutes to get up to Overlook Point. Chance was glad that the road was clear. He hadn't driven out this way in years.

Hope peered out the window into the darkness. "I'm guessing it's really pretty out here?"

"If you ask me, it's the most beautiful spot in the whole valley, and that's saying something."

She smiled. "It's a pity we can't see it then really, isn't it?"

"We will. I know patience isn't one of your virtues, but one thing I can guarantee you is that the sun is going to rise right over that ridge soon."

"Ooh. I need more coffee. I'm obviously not awake yet. It hadn't even registered that we'd come to see the sun rise." She leaned across and kissed his cheek. "That is so sweet of you."

He narrowed his eyes at her.

"Seriously! It is. I'm not just saying that to get a rise out of you," she said with a smile.

He nodded grudgingly. "I know. You wouldn't dare."

Her smile faded. "Maybe I would. I used to think you'd never make a promise, but now I know I was wrong about that."

"You have no idea how wrong we both were about that." Chance held her gaze for a moment, tempted to ask her right here and now. He wanted her to know that when the two of them got married, that would be the most important promise of his life. And more than that, he wanted her to know that it was a promise he wanted to make.

She stared back at him, waiting for him to say more, but there was a doubt, or something in her eyes, that convinced him he should wait. He should do this the way he'd imagined. He wanted it to be special for her, and there were things he wanted to say. Things that would be best said when the sun rose.

Chapter Sixteen

All the stars slowly fade as the sky gets lighter, then comes the glow and then finally, the sun comes up and ushers in the new day and a whole new beginning.

Chance made her sit inside the truck while he went back in the bed and set things up for them. She smiled as she sipped on her coffee. This was a great way to start a Sunday morning, even if he had dragged her out of bed at the crack of sparrow fart to get here. No matter what he might say, he was sweet and thoughtful. Only yesterday she'd told him how much she loved to watch the sunrise and now here they were in the most beautiful spot in the valley, ready to usher in a new day.

Chance pulled her door open and grinned at her. "Are you ready?"

"I am. Do I need one of those coats?"

"Nah, I'll keep you warm." He scooped her out of her seat and she managed to cling to him and her coffee as he carried her around and set her down in the bed of the truck.

"What do you think?" He looked as eager as a kid hoping to please.

"This is absolutely wonderful! Why haven't we done this before?" He'd set up a bed back here, with a foam mattress and a duvet and a pile of pillows. "I love it! Come on in!" She crawled up to the top and propped the pillows against the cab so they could lean back on them.

Chance scrambled after her and pulled the duvet up around them. He put his arm around her shoulders and smiled down at her.

She smiled back. "This is perfect, Chance!"

The sky was starting to lighten now, and if she didn't know better, she'd think the shine in his eyes might be tears?

"You think?"

She nodded vigorously. "It is, just perfect. You might joke around, but you do have a little romantic streak in there somewhere, don't you?"

"Maybe, but I think it's a pretty narrow streak. I've never found it before."

She laughed. "Well, you have now. You've totally blown me away with this." She looked up at the stars. "Do you remember what I told you yesterday about what I love about watching the sunrise?"

He nodded solemnly. "Every word."

She chuckled. "What did I say about the stars, then?"

"Don't laugh. You're not going to catch me out. I remember it all, it's why we're here. You said that the stars slowly fade when the sky gets lighter, then there's the glow, and then finally, the sun comes up and ushers in the new day and a whole new beginning."

"Wow! I think that's word for word."

He nodded. "After you went to sleep last night, I did a lot of thinking. Especially about what you said about how we react to things being a choice. I'm going to work on that. I'm going to learn to choose more wisely. I want to be a fun, happy guy. Not someone who's always caught up in the negatives."

"Aww, you're not like that. I wasn't criticizing you. I was trying to help. I take the attitude I do because it helps me feel better, that's all. I wanted you to feel better, too."

"I know, and you made me see that I can feel better. I don't want to dwell on the past and the pain anymore. I want to look to the future. Our future. What you said about the stars slowly fading away?" He looked up into the sky and she followed his gaze. It was happening right now, the stars that had been shining so brightly while they drove up here seemed paler now as the sky lightened.

She nodded. "Yeah?"

"Well, that's why I wanted us to come here this morning and watch it happen. You said the sunrise is a new beginning. I want this morning to be our new beginning, Hope." His voice was gruff and she looked at him more closely. Maybe those were tears in his eyes. He shook his head. "Let me finish?" he croaked. "I'm going to be blubbing like a baby soon and I want to get this out first."

She nodded and found his hand under the duvet and squeezed it.

"I want us to watch the stars fade away and let them go. The stars are like the past. When a new day comes, the stars are still there, but we don't see them anymore. That's how the past should be. It's part of us; it'll always be there, but in the background. The stars can't outshine the daylight."

She felt her own eyes prick with tears. Was this his way of saying he was ready to let Chloe go? They'd never talked about the past without him mentioning her name. She didn't think that it was just her imagination that he was deliberately talking about the past and not Chloe.

He squeezed his arm tighter around her shoulders and when she looked up at him, his mouth came down on hers. It was a tender kiss. It tasted of tears, though she wasn't sure whose. It didn't matter—they were good tears, happy tears. That much she did know.

When he finally lifted his head, he smiled. "Damn, I'm good!"

She laughed. "And modest, too. Though I won't argue, you are a great kisser."

"No! I meant my timing. Look." He jerked his head at the skyline where a crimson glow was starting to creep its way up above the mountains.

"It's beautiful."

"It is, and it's the next thing you described. To me, it's what happens when you let the stars fade away. You get a warm, happy glow and you're free, free to step into the new day—into the future."

"Wow! You really are good. You've got me all teary-eyed again here."

He smiled. "Are you ready to start a new day with me, Hope?"

She nodded, understanding that there was more significance to his question than if she was ready to watch the sun rise. "I am. I want to step into every new day with you."

"Honey," he fumbled around under the duvet and pulled something out. "I love you. I wanted to come up with some big fancy proposal for you, but I couldn't, it's not me." He looked down into her eyes. "I love you with all my heart and soul. I want to spend the rest of my life with you, I want to be the best man I can be for you. I'm already a better man because of you. Damn! All I'm really trying to say is, will you marry me?"

Her eyes filled with tears and she tried to blink them away as she nodded. "Yes! Yes, please, Chance. Nothing would make me happier."

He fumbled to open the box and held it out to her. "We can change it if you don't like it."

"Chance, it's gorgeous!" It really was. It was an exquisite princess cut diamond set in a plain gold band. He looked so uncertain; she took the box from him and took the ring out. "Are you going to put it on me?" She gave him the ring and held out her left hand.

He looked up at the horizon as he took hold of her finger and smiled. There was a bright halo above the mountain where the sun was starting to rise. "See. This is how I wanted it to be. I wanted to put this on you at the moment the sun came up. You said, finally, the sun comes up and ushers in the new day and a whole new beginning. That's what I want this moment to be for us, Hope. A new day, and a whole new beginning."

She nodded through the tears as he slid the ring onto her finger. "It is, this is the beginning of the rest of our lives, Chance. And we're going to spend them together, making each other happy."

He smiled and looked at the ring on her finger. "Does it fit?"

"Perfectly. However you guessed my size, it worked."

He chuckled. "I'll tell you about it some time, but right now, I just want us to sit and watch the sun come up." He tightened his arm around her shoulders and she rested her head against him. He was right; this moment was too special to be telling stories about the ring. There'd be plenty of other times for that. This moment, this sunrise, this new beginning would only ever happen once and she, like he, wanted to savor every moment of it.

~ ~ ~

The sun was well clear of the mountains before they spoke again. Chance turned and dropped a kiss on her lips. This was exactly how he'd wanted it to be, he just hoped it was right for her. No, he knew, he could tell, it was perfect for her.

She smiled up at him. "Can I ask you something?"

"Anything?"

"You know marriage is a promise, right?"

"Shit!"

Her smile disappeared and he had to laugh. "Sorry, my timing wasn't so perfect on that one. I didn't mean that how it sounded. It's just that I forgot most of what I wanted to say in my proposal. I needed to get the bit about the sunrise right. I meant, shit that I was so focused on it, that I forgot the rest. I wanted to tell you about the promise, too. I already told you that I'm over that, and I am. It's a part of the past and I've let it go. I don't think I'll ever make a promise lightly, but when we get married, when I say I do, that'll be the biggest, most important promise I ever make. The one that means the most to me. I need you to understand that."

She smiled. "Thank you. I do now. That had been worrying me."

"How?"

She shrugged. "I feel stupid about it now, but I was starting to think that maybe you didn't want to marry me, because it is a promise. The most important promise."

"I'm sorry, honey. I hate that you thought I didn't want you to be my wife. I screwed up big time over asking you. I wanted to, but I couldn't figure out how to do it. I left it too long and I'm sorry."

She smiled. "You didn't leave it too long at all. This was perfect, it was the right time, in the right place."

"I wanted it to be. I wanted to get it right."

"Well, you did, and you got the ring right, too. I love it."

He smiled. "I'm glad. It has to be right, you're going to wear it for the rest of your life."

"I am. I'll wear your ring and I'll be Hope Malone."

"You will?"

"Of course!"

"You don't have to change your name, if you don't want. You're a Davenport." He had to wonder what her dad would make of it.

"I'm going to be a Malone. I know some women want to keep their maiden name, but I want to take yours. It's important to me."

"Okay. It's your choice, honey."

"It is." Her smile faded. "I don't know if Dad will like it."

Chance chuckled. "Mind reader."

"It's not his decision to make. He'll just have to like it or lump it."

"I guess, but if you don't mind, I'm going to stay out of that one."

She laughed. "Coward."

"Nope. I'm smart, that's all."

"I can't wait to tell him. We should tell him first, if that's okay with you? Him and your dad and Alice, and Dave and Monique, we should tell them before we tell anyone else."

Chance had to smile. "Do you mind if we add Missy to that list? I might not be much use to you as a husband if she hears it from someone else before she hears it from us."

Hope laughed. "Of course. She should be one of the first, and the Remington brothers, too. I was just thinking about parents first."

"I know. Do you want to get back and call your dad?"

"I do." She ran her hand up his leg under the duvet, making his cock spring to attention, "but there's something else I'd like to do first."

He turned to face her and nipped her bottom lip as he slid them down to a lying position. "Oh, yeah? And what might that be?"

Her fingers were working on his buckle, trying to get him out of his jeans. He had a much easier time pushing her pajamas down. She got him unfastened and slid her hand inside his boxers, cupping him and sending shivers chasing each other down his spine. "My fiancé," she said with a smile. "I want to do you." She shook her head. "Actually, that's not true. I don't want to do you. I want you to make love to me. I don't know if you remember that first night I was here and we met at Mill Creek. We were in so much of a hurry to get each other into bed, I suggested we climb into the back of your truck. You said the truck could wait till summer came around. I hoped then that we'd still be together when summer came. Now it's here and not only are we together, but we're engaged. I've waited a long time for this, but it means so much more now. Back then we were in lust, now we know we're in love and I want to make love to you."

Chance pushed his jeans down and kicked his feet out of them while she spoke. She was right, this shouldn't be a quickie. It was special. They should take their time, and do it right.

When they were both naked, she held her arms up to him and he bent his head to kiss her. She pulled him down and slid his arm under her. He loved the way her full, soft breasts felt against his chest. He ran his hand down her side and she trembled under his touch. That fascinated him and he did it again, feeling the goose bumps that dappled her soft skin. He'd never focused on just simple touch before. Usually, he was touching her in all the right places, knowing what turned her on. This was different. Her arousal wasn't the result of inserting Tab A in Hole B; it was more than that. It was love and trust. And it worked both ways, he realized as her fingers tangled in his hair and his scalp tingled. This wasn't physical loving—it was heart and soul loving.

He ran his hand down her side one more time, then carried on to cup it around her ass. She gasped in the same way she usually did when he slid his fingers inside her. Damn! He was going to have to learn more about this kind of loving. He'd thought he'd been focusing on the important stuff, but it seemed he might have been missing the point entirely.

They were lying face to face and she slid her hand between them and brought her leg up around his hip. Her fingers curled around him and guided him into her warmth. Chance closed his eyes and let the sensations roll through him. This was amazing. He wasn't inside her, they weren't even moving, but he was as aroused as he'd ever been. She kissed him, flicking her tongue inside his mouth. His hand came up into her hair and pulled her head back as he devoured her mouth. His hips were moving against hers of their own accord now. The need to be inside her, for their bodies to become one, was overwhelming now.

She turned on her back, taking him with her and opening her legs to him. He positioned himself above her and smiled as the duvet slid down and the cool morning air touched his back. She was beautiful, her bare skin glowing in the golden light of the sun's early rays.

She ran her hands up his arms and smiled. "Make love to me, Chance."

He didn't need telling twice. He held her gaze as he thrust his hips hard.

"Chance!" she gasped as he entered her.

"Hope," he breathed as he began to move inside her. She was his Hope and his hope. The words and the emotions all mingled together as his mind drifted away and his body took over. She brought her legs up around his back as he thrust over and over again into her velvety wetness. Her inner muscles gripped him tight, pulsating around him, carrying him toward the point of no return. Her cheeks were flushed and her breasts bounced as he picked up the pace. He was driving her toward her orgasm, their momentum gathering like a runaway train. He felt as if his blood were boiling in his veins and there was only one inevitable conclusion.

"Yes," she gasped and he felt her tense around him. He thrust deeper and harder with every stroke, eliciting her encouragement as a, "Yes, yes, oh, God! Chance! Yesss!"

"Yes!" He agreed as the floodgates within him opened and all the pressure that had been building in his veins found its release deep inside her. She milked him for everything he had to give, her hips bucking wildly like a young filly he knew would give in to him if he could just stay on top of her long enough. He pushed up on his hands and arched his back as he finished her off. She screamed and dug her nails into his ass, which sent a whole new wave of sensations crashing though him and emptying into her. He thought he'd come all he could, but as she scratched her fingernails over his ass cheeks, he found he still had more to give and she took it willingly.

When they finally stilled, he rolled off her and she snuggled into his side. "I can't think of any other way I'd rather begin our new life together," she murmured.

"Me neither."

She smiled up at him. "Maybe we should make that our new tradition—the best way to start the day?"

He chuckled. "I'd love to, but I'd hate to have to wake you up for it every morning before I go to work."

She shrugged. "I don't mind, it's worth it."

He shook his head at her. "You're a sensual woman, Hope."

"I guess. I never thought I was until I met you."

That made him smile. "Aww, now I feel special."

"That's because you are special, very special. You're a wonderful man, Chance, and soon, you're going to be my husband."

"And soon, you're going to be my wife."

"I can't wait."

His smile faded. "What do you want to do about a wedding? The when and the where and the how, and everything? I don't want to make it all your responsibility, but I'm guessing all that stuff will be important to you, in a way that ..." He didn't want to say it wasn't important to him.

She smiled. "Don't worry. We'll figure it out. I want us to do something that will work for us both. I do want you to be involved, but I don't want you to feel like you have to get swamped under a whole load of details that don't interest you."

He smiled. She really did understand him. "Thanks, honey."

Chapter Seventeen

Back at the cabin, they showered and got dressed, ready to face the day, before they started making their phone calls.

"Do you want to call your dad and I'll call mine?" asked Chance.

"Would you mind if we call them together? I'd like to hear your dad's reaction, and I'm sure mine will want to talk to you, as well."

"Yeah, sorry. You're right. I was just trying to avoid the question of who we call first."

"I've already decided it should be your dad. He's been waiting and waiting for this. It's only fair."

Chance smiled and came to give her a kiss. "Thanks."

"It's not just for you. It's important to me, too."

"I know, that's what I'm thanking you for—for caring, for being you."

She shrugged. "I can't help being me. It comes naturally. Let's get on with it. It's going to take us a while to call everyone we need to. We'd better get started."

They took their coffees outside to the back porch and Chance dialed the number and hit the speaker button before laying the phone down on the table.

Hope opened her mouth, but he answered the question before she could ask it. "You can be the one to tell him, if you want."

"Thanks."

"Hello?"

"Hi, Alice. You're on speaker with me and Hope."

"Oh, good morning, kids. Hang on, let me get your dad. Frank! It's Chance and Hope."

They smiled at each other as they heard a mumbled conversation on the other end of the line, and the phone rustling before Frank's voice came through loud and clear.

"What do you two want on a Sunday morning? I thought you'd still be in bed."

Chance chuckled. "Morning, Dad; it's nice to talk to you, too. We can hang up and leave you to it, if you're busy."

"I didn't say that!"

"He's only teasing," said Hope.

"I know. I can ignore him. How are you, young lady?"

"I'm doing great; thanks, Frank. In fact, I couldn't be happier. Is Alice still there?"

"I'm here, sweetie," called Alice.

"Good, because there's something we want to tell you both …"

"You're getting married?" Frank's voice rose into a croak as he asked the question.

"We are, and we wanted you to be the first to know."

"Congratulations!" called Alice.

"About bloody time, too," said Frank.

Hope grinned at Chance. "The best things in life are worth waiting for, Dad. You know that."

"Ay, son. You're right about that, and you sure did find yourself the best. I'm happy for you, both of you. I might give him a hard time, Hope, but I can tell you, you've got yourself a fine man there."

Hope's eyes filled with tears as she watched Chance cover his eyes and turn away. She knew they'd had a tough time with each other over the years, so to hear his dad say that must mean the world to him. "Oh, I know it," she said. "I'm a lucky lady."

"You are that," said Frank. "And he's one lucky son of a gun to have you. You're perfect for each other."

"Thank you. We think so."

"I'm so happy for you both," said Alice. "Have you told Missy?"

"No," said Chance. "We will, but we both wanted you to be the very first ones to know."

Frank's voice sounded hoarse again. "Aww, thanks, son. That means a lot."

"It means a lot to me, too, Dad."

"Hope, have you had any thoughts about your wedding yet?" asked Alice. "We probably need something to talk about while these two dry their eyes."

Hope chuckled. "Not yet, no. He only just asked me this morning. I'll keep you posted with whatever we decide, though. And don't forget, you don't need to worry about traveling, or about where you'll stay. We'll take care of it all."

"Thanks, sweetie. You've given me something to look forward to. I'll have to start looking for a new frock."

Hope looked at Chance. He was still recovering his composure, and besides, she didn't need to ask his permission. Alice was going to be her family too, now. "If you'd like, we can go shopping together? I'll come down there and we can go wherever you want."

"Ooh. I ..." began Alice.

"You hear that, Chance?" Frank interrupted. "They're going shopping together now."

"That's all right, Dad. I'll come hang with you when they do. We can go fishing or something."

"You've got yourself a deal, son."

"Sounds good to me, Alice," said Hope. "If they're fishing, they won't notice how long we're gone."

"Sounds good to me, too," said Alice with a giggle, and for the first time, Hope thought about her as a woman like herself. A woman who'd somehow met and fallen in love with a grumpy, lonely man. It made her wonder if Alice was happy, and if she had friends or fun in her life.

"Maybe we should make it a regular thing?" Hope suggested.

Chance raised an eyebrow at her, but she smiled and nodded. She'd like to do it.

"I'd like that," said Alice.

"Thanks for calling us," said Frank. "Congratulations to the both of you. I'll bet you need to get us off the line now so you can call everyone else, don't you?"

"Yeah, we should," said Chance.

"Don't worry, son. You know I'm not a big talker. You've told me what I've been waiting to hear, and it means the world that you called us first. So, go on. Go call around, but be sure not to forget Missy. I won't be able to talk to her till you do."

Chance smiled. "We will, but we need to call Hope's dad first."

"Give him my best."

"Will do."

"Bye, Frank; Bye, Alice," called Hope.

Once she'd hung up, she smiled at Chance. "I'm so glad we told him first."

"Yeah, thanks for doing that."

"I wanted to, but now I want to talk to my dad, too."

"Of course. Do you want to put him on speaker, or would you rather talk to him privately?"

"No! I want us both to tell him." Hope wanted him to feel as close to her dad as she did to his—even if she knew that'd take a while.

Chance smiled. "Okay, good. I was hoping you'd say that."

"Are you ready?" When he nodded, she took her phone out and dialed the number, then just like he had, she hit the speaker button and laid the phone down on the table.

"Good morning, Hopey. What are you up to today? I'm cooking again. I'm trying out a casserole and I made an extra one. If it turns out well, I thought I might stop by the cabin and bring it for you and Chance."

Hope's heart melted a little. Was this really the same cold, distant man whom she'd barely talked to in the years since her mom died? Chance cocked his head to one side and made a little aww sound, reminding her that yes, it really was possible for a man to change so much in such a short time. "That'd be lovely. Thank you. Listen, you're on speaker with me and Chance."

"Oh. Good morning, Chance. Don't bank on having casserole for dinner, will you? It might turn out to be inedible."

Chance chuckled. "You never know. It might be great."

"Anything's possible, I suppose. Anyway, what's going on?"

Hope smiled. "We have news."

"You do?"

"Yes." She looked at Chance. He seemed relaxed and happy, not at all nervous about what her dad might say. "Chance asked me to marry him, and I said yes. We're getting married, Dad!"

"That's wonderful news! Congratulations!"

"Thank you," said Chance.

"Have you had any thoughts about your wedding?"

Hope shot a quick glance at Chance. "Not yet, no. I don't want anything big, though—just family and close friends."

"Don't worry, Hopey. I wasn't going to try to turn it into some big event for the rich and famous."

"I know." To be fair, she had been concerned for a minute there that, as his only child, he might want to throw a big wedding for her.

"I was just wondering …" Uh-oh, she looked at Chance, but he didn't seem worried what he might be about to say. "I wondered if … It's just a thought, and probably not a good one, but would you want to hold it here?"

She looked at Chance, who shrugged. She had been thinking they'd probably get married here in the valley.

"I mean, at the house."

"Oh." She looked at Chance again and he held his hands open and nodded, in a gesture that said whatever she wanted was good by him. "Maybe," she said. "I'd have to think about it, see how I feel. How would you feel, Dad?"

"I'd be proud. I can't lie, it would be emotional. Wherever you get married, I'll be emotional, but if you want to do it here …" His voice trailed off.

"I know. I feel the same way. Maybe it's a good idea, or maybe it would feel too sad. Let me think about it?"

"Of course. It was only a suggestion. What do you think, Chance?"

"I think it could be an awesome idea. It could feel right, but at the same time, it could make for a bittersweet day for you. I think you should think about it, the same as Hope."

"You're right, of course, but what about you? How would it be for you?"

Chance smiled. "I'm fine with wherever we do it. I don't have any expectations of the day itself. Not for me. As far as I'm concerned, it's all about Hope. I'm looking forward to the wedding; but honestly, I care more about the being married part than the getting married part." He gave Hope an apologetic shrug—as if he were telling her something she didn't already know!

"Spoken like a true man," said her dad. "Just know that whatever you decide, whatever you want, will be wonderful in my eyes. And, Chance?"

"Yes?"

"Since you've already honored one tradition. Would you be so gracious as to allow me to honor another?"

She could see the struggle on Chance's face. She wasn't sure what her dad meant, but she knew he'd worded his request so carefully that it'd be hard for Chance to say no.

Chance smiled ruefully. "I guess you outplayed me on that one, huh? Since it would be ungracious of me to refuse, then yes, and thank you."

"No, thank you."

The sound of her dad's laughter made her smile, even though she didn't understand what was going on. "Is anyone going to explain it to me?" she asked.

"When Chance came to ask me for your hand in marriage, I understood that he is a traditionalist at heart. Or at least, he wanted to honor the tradition. My question was whether he would be comfortable in allowing me to uphold the tradition of the family of the bride paying for the wedding."

"Oh!" She looked at Chance and he shrugged. She didn't even know he'd asked her dad's permission. She was glad her dad had played it this way. She knew he would want to pay for everything, and she also knew that Chance might be uncomfortable with it. But framing it as a tradition to be honored had put him in a position where he couldn't really say no.

Her dad chuckled. "And on that note, I'm going to have to get back to my casserole. I'm sure you have other calls you want to make. If I produce something edible, I'll give you a call later, and see if you want me to deliver it for you."

"Thanks, Dad."

After she'd hung up, she raised an eyebrow at Chance. "I didn't know you'd asked his permission."

Chance smiled. "Well, you're not supposed to know, are you? It doesn't work that way. I couldn't exactly tell you I was going to ask him."

She laughed. "No, sorry, that was a bit dumb of me. What I should have said is that I'm amazed and grateful that you did that."

He nodded. "It was the right thing to do. I'm glad I did."

"Me too. So, who do you want to call next?"

Chance shrugged. "Dave and Monique and Missy are next on my list, then the guys, but what about you?"

"I want to call Toby, he's the closest thing I have to a brother, or a friend."

"Yeah, you should call him. I like him. Do you think he'll come to the wedding?"

She laughed. "Slow down, would you? We haven't even decided when the wedding is going to be, let alone where."

He frowned. "Oh, yeah. Details, huh? I guess we should work them out."

"We should, but let's get done with telling everyone first. Should we call Dave and Monique next?"

"Yeah." He called their number and waited while it rang. Monique picked up. Hope loved her. "Chance?"

"Yep, me and Hope, we're on the speaker. Is Dave with you?"

"Yes. Let me put the speaker on my phone also. Okay. Dave. It's Chance and Hope. Say hello."

"Hey. Is everything all right?"

"Couldn't be better," said Chance.

"Hello!" called Hope.

"We have something to tell you; that's why we're calling on a Sunday morning."

"Oh, yeah? What's that?" Hope could hear the smile in Dave's voice. He already knew what was coming and so did Monique, by the sound of it.

"Tell us the good news!" she said in an excited voice.

Chance chuckled. "I'm sure you've already guessed, but I just asked this wonderful woman to be my wife, and she accepted."

"We're getting married," said Hope.

"That's wonderful. Congratulations!" said Dave.

"Ça c'est magnifique!" cried Monique. "I'm so very, very happy for you both. Hope, you have to know that I worried for years about my lucky Chance."

Hope smiled; she hadn't heard that one before. Chance rolled his eyes.

"We all did," added Dave. "I used to think he was destined to be the lonely old cowboy."

"But I prayed for more. I knew there was a special lady out there for him," said Monique. "He found you."

Dave chuckled. "The first time we met you, I knew he'd found Hope."

Chance groaned. "I thought you'd be the last one to start with the word plays."

Dave chuckled. "Sorry, it's just too tempting. It's got to be done. And I have one more for you both."

"Go on, what is it?" Chance pursed his lips at Hope and she chuckled. He might pretend to get tired of people playing with their names, but he loved it, really.

"You both have to remember to give hope a chance."

Hope smiled. "Oh, that's a new one! I love it, thank you."

"I have one too," said Monique.

"Go on, you may as well jump on the bandwagon," said Chance. "What's yours?"

"It's a, what's the word? An acronym, that's it. Hope, is an acronym."

Chance raised an eyebrow at her, but Hope shrugged. She'd never heard of one.

"You know, where the letters are all the first letter of another word? Hope means: Hold On, Pain Ends."

Hope smiled. "Oh, that's lovely. I've never heard that before. Have you, Chance?"

"No." He smiled, but he didn't look happy.

"I hope it is true for you," said Monique.

"Thanks."

Chance made the right noises until they got off the phone, but he wasn't right. Once they'd hung up, Hope turned to him. "What is it?"

He shrugged. "Nothing. I'm just being dumb. Let's get on and call Miss and the others, huh?"

"Okay." She didn't want to push him. There'd been times when she'd asked him for a bit of leeway when she was reacting to something badly; when she knew she was being too emotional, but still needed a bit of time to get past it.

They spent most of the rest of the morning on the phone, sharing their news with Missy and the Remingtons and Toby. Hope tried not to dwell too much on the fact that the only person she wanted to call was the guy who used to work for her. Yes, he'd become a dear friend over the years, but she'd never even have met him if she hadn't hired him.

"Is there anyone else we want to tell?" she asked when they got off the phone with Shane and Cassidy.

Chance shrugged. "Not that I can think of."

"Well, I can think of someone, but it's someone of yours."

"Who?"

For a second, she wondered if he was deliberately being obtuse, but he didn't do that. As big as calling Renée was in her mind, it seemed it wasn't such a big deal to him.

"Don't look at me like that. If it's someone important, then I'm sorry, but I'm drawing a blank here."

"No, I'm not mad that you've forgotten someone! I'm just feeling weird that I want to call her, but it seems you don't."

"Who?"

"Renée!"

"Oh!"

"Yeah. I'm sorry. I shouldn't have brought it up, especially if it wasn't on your mind in the first place."

He shook his head. "It wasn't, but you're right. I'd like to tell her."

"I would, too."

"You're not just playing that whole thing up because you think it's important to me?"

"No. It's important to me. I like her, a lot. I want to share our news with her. She's a part of your past who's still around to be in your present." She shrugged. "I don't know what else to say."

Chance got up from his seat and came to squat in front of her. He rested his hands on her knees and looked deep into her eyes. "I love you, honey."

She cupped his face in her hands and planted a kiss on his lips. "And I love you, Chancey bear." He narrowed his eyes at her, but she laughed. "Every time you call me honey, it makes me think about how bears love honey, and you're my Chancey bear."

He groaned.

"You should be grateful I don't say it every time I think it, or you'd be hearing it several times a day, every day."

"Okay, I guess I can at least be grateful for that."

She smiled. "There you go. I know you said you're trying to look for the bright side more than focusing on the downside. You're getting there. That's progress."

He nodded grimly. "I'm glad you noticed. I'll tell you one thing I haven't managed to find a bright side for yet."

"What's that?"

"That damned photographer last night."

She sighed. "No, I haven't found a bright side for that yet myself. I hate it, if I'm honest. I've been able to put it out of my mind all morning, but it's still there like a dark cloud on the horizon."

Chance nodded. "I think it's more likely to brew up into a thunderstorm than go away. No matter how I try to spin it in my mind."

"I know, and you're probably right, but we can't do anything about it until it happens."

"I guess, but I'm afraid it's going to happen at the worst time."

"What do you mean?"

"Aren't we about to start planning our wedding?"

"Yeah." She sighed. "But we can't let the thought of press intrusion affect us. We just have to get on and do what we're going to do."

"Do you have any idea what you want to do—or when?"

"No. I haven't had much time to process it yet. What about you? You've had a bit longer than I have. When are you thinking?"

He shrugged. "Like you said, I'm such a guy. I'd be happy to get someone out here this afternoon who could say a few words, I'd put a ring on your finger, you'd put one on mine and we'd be done."

Hope smiled. "That sounds like a plan to me."

"No. You deserve more than that. A woman should have the wedding she wants, but we've never talked about what you want. The when will depend on how long it all takes to organize, but I'd like us to do it soon. I don't want to wait too long."

"Neither do I. I think I would like to have the wedding at Dad's house." She'd been thinking about it since they spoke to him earlier and it felt right. "If that's okay with you?"

"It is. I think it's a good idea. It's right."

"Okay, so we know where, how about we say the when is as soon as we can make it happen?"

He grinned. "I'm in."

Chapter Eighteen

Chance checked the clock on the dash when he pulled into Shane and Cassidy's driveway. They were right on time.

"Sorry I held us up," said Hope.

"We made it, it's not a problem," he said with a smile.

She'd been working with her dad all day every day for a couple of weeks now. He was happy to see her enjoying herself so much—and from what she'd shown him, she was doing very well for herself. He'd had no idea that people could make that kind of money in a day.

"I know, but I shouldn't have stayed at Dad's so long. It was only because we had the caterers over this afternoon to work on the menu for the reception. Then when we got back to work, I got a bit carried away."

He pulled up in front of the house and leaned across to kiss her lips. "It's okay. I'm glad you're enjoying yourself, and you shouldn't feel bad that you're taking time to plan our wedding. I feel bad that I haven't done anything, and I don't even know what I could do."

"You just need to show up," she said with a smile. "Just be there, say you love me and that you want to spend the rest of your life with me, and I'll be the happiest girl on earth. If you cared in the slightest about the food or the flowers or any of that, then I'd be trying to include you. But since you don't, I'm just getting on with it."

Chance felt bad. "It shouldn't have to all fall on your shoulders."

"I don't mind. I'm realistic about it. I could try to get you involved, but that would be wasting both of our time for very little benefit. None of those details matter to you, and I enjoy it and can get on with it."

"Okay, I know you're right. There is one thing I want us to do together, though."

"What's that?"

"Pick the wedding rings. Laura has an online store now and she sent me a link so that we can look at her collection. It doesn't matter if we don't like any of hers, but I thought you'd want to look since she made your engagement ring, and she might have something nice to match it."

Hope held her hand up and admired the ring. "Yes, I'd love to see what she has. I love this so much."

Chance smiled, glad that he'd gotten it right—with Laura's help.

The front door opened and Shane came out. "Come on!" he called. "I've been waiting for you to get here."

"How does he do that?" asked Hope. "How does he know when we arrive?"

Chance laughed. "They have a camera system with a monitor in the hall, so he can see when we come up the driveway."

"Oh, okay. I thought he just had some weird instinct about when we arrive—either that or supersensitive hearing."

They got out of the truck and Shane held the door open for them when they reached the top of the steps. "Come on in. You're not the last. Gina and Mason just left the ranch a few minutes ago; it shouldn't take them long."

"Hey, guys. Don't let him harass you, you can come join me in the kitchen, if you want. I have wine."

Shane grinned at them. "I have beer, if that'll tempt you out onto the deck with me?"

Chance looked at Hope.

"How about you go that way, and I'll go that way?" She pointed to the kitchen and he nodded.

Shane punched his shoulder and went to the wet bar in the family room to get him a beer. "It's good to see you're not under the thumb yet."

Chance laughed. "What, not like you?"

Shane laughed with him. "Nah, we can joke all we like, but I think we got damned lucky that we found women who wouldn't want us under their thumbs, or under their feet. We'd get in the way of what they want to do for themselves."

"That's so true. I can't imagine being with a woman who wanted me to be by her side the whole time."

Shane shook his head. "Nope. Me neither, but it's not something we'll ever have to worry about. Come on outside. Carter's out there by himself."

"Where's Summer?"

"In the kitchen with Cassidy. She's another one who doesn't need her man by her side the whole time. Although, I think Carter would like to be."

Chance smiled as he followed Shane outside. He was right, Carter probably would go everywhere with Summer, if she'd let him. He was like her bodyguard.

"Hey, Chance."

"Carter. How's it going?"

"Yep, everything's good in my world. How about you?"

"Couldn't be better."

"How's the wedding planning coming?"

Shane laughed. "You should probably be in the kitchen if you want to hear about that."

Carter made a face. "I'm not asking what color flowers they're having. I care about how he feels in the middle of it all."

Chance smiled. "I feel great. Hope's taking care of most of it and I'm just joining in on the chorus, when she needs me."

Shane nodded approvingly, but Carter frowned.

"It's okay, Big C. I'm useless with that kind of thing and she enjoys it. I've offered and offered to do more, be more involved, but she knows me and she knows herself. It's all good."

Carter's smile returned. "In that case, it sounds perfect. Have you had any more trouble with the press?"

"No. I'm still looking over my shoulder the whole time, but since that one guy, there's been no sign of any more."

"Good, you don't need them showing up and spoiling things for you."

"Who's spoiling things?" asked Cassidy as she came out the sliding door from the kitchen.

"No one, hopefully," said Chance.

"The press, if they show up and start harassing him and Hope again," said Shane.

Cassidy made a face. "They're bottom feeders, if you ask me. All of them."

"You won't get any arguments from me," said Carter.

"That's not fair," said Chance. "I have as much reason to hate them as anyone, but they're just doing their job. I don't understand what would motivate anyone to do that job, but …"

Shane looked at him. "Are you going soft in your old age?"

Cassidy laughed. "It's not old age; it's love that's mellowing him out. Right, Chance?"

He nodded. It was. If he didn't love Hope, he might never have tried to change his approach to life. He was still working on it. It wasn't easy, but he was catching himself when he was being negative and trying to turn things around to find the bright side.

Shane gave him a skeptical look. "I wonder if you'll still be this mellow when they come poking their cameras in your face again. Steve told me he was lucky to get that photographer out of there before you beat him to a pulp."

Chance scowled. He didn't like that they still thought of him as the guy who would do that. Yeah, he'd been about to hit the guy, but he would have floored him with one good punch. He wouldn't have beaten him to a pulp. He hated that expression, mostly because it was pretty much what he'd done to Kyle all those years ago.

Hope appeared in the doorway behind Cassidy, a glass of wine in her hand. "I think Steve was exaggerating a bit. Chance never raised his fist, and Steve wasn't there that fast."

Chance nodded at her with a grateful smile. She knew; she understood he was trying to be better than that.

Shane gave him an apologetic smile. "I'm glad to hear it." He turned at the sound of a buzzer going off inside. "That'll be Gina and Mase. I'll go let them in."

~ ~ ~

Hope looked around the table as they ate. They were a great bunch of people. The guys were all handsome in their own way, but more than their looks, they shared a way of being, a set of underlying principles that she liked. They were good, hard-working men who each had a big heart and a great sense of humor. It was unusual for them all to be quiet, but then that probably had a lot to do with the lasagna they were eating. It was amazing.

"This is so good, Cassidy," she said.

Cassidy smiled. "Thanks. It's a recipe my dad's wife gave me, and these guys love it. It's the standard request now whenever Shane and I host dinner."

Beau looked at Chance. "That's a thought; are the two of you going to take a turn hosting when you're married?"

Chance shot a look at her. "I don't know, you'll have to ask the boss if she's interested. If it's up to me, all you'll get is meat straight from the grill."

Hope smiled. "I'd love to, but we might have to wait until we get a house built."

Mason smiled at her. "If you'll have us, we'd love to come, no matter where you are or even if we'll all fit inside. It's summer, we can sit out back."

Corinne nodded at her. "Beau and I hosted in the cabin at the guest ranch before we got our place built."

"Okay, then. I'd love to. I love to cook, but it might have to wait until after the wedding. I'm crazy busy at the moment."

"Whenever you're ready," said Gina. "It's not a hurry up and invite us over, it's a we want you to feel like part of the family."

Beau smiled at her. "I can vouch for that. I was the black sheep of the family for years, but when they started having these dinners and inviting me along, I started to feel like I belonged. Then, when Corinne and I started taking a turn to host, it made me feel I was fully back in the family again."

"Aww, isn't he sweet?" asked Chance.

Hope smiled. She liked Beau and Corinne, although she didn't know them as well as the others yet. "It sounds like we'll be following in your footsteps, then—including building a house."

"Yeah, what's the plan with that?" asked Mason.

"We're working on it," said Chance. "While Hope's setting up the wedding, I'm doing the legwork so that we'll be able to build when we're ready." He turned to Hope. "We're going to ride out this weekend and see if we can pick the perfect spot."

She smiled back and nodded happily. That was no doubt what he'd wanted to tell her when she got back from her dad's earlier, but hadn't had time because she'd been so late.

"Do you have your guest list and everything figured out yet for the wedding?" asked Summer.

"We do. It's not very big. We only want family, and Chance's friends from Summer Lake are coming, too."

Summer nodded, and if Hope didn't know any better, she'd think she looked a little put out. She couldn't understand why, though, so she let it go.

"And what about your wedding party?" asked Cassidy. "Do you know who you're going to ask to be in it?" She grinned. "I haven't heard anything yet."

"Cassidy!" Gina shook her head. "Take no notice of her. Cassidy thinks she has to be at the center of everything."

Hope laughed. "I don't mind. That's one thing we still need to figure out."

Chance nodded. "We're working on it."

She knew it was bothering him. How was he supposed to choose only one of his four brothers to be his best man? She didn't know what to do. She liked all the girls; she'd known them all for the same amount of time. How could she ask one or two of them to be her bridesmaid, but not the others? And how could she ask all of them? And there was Missy. As Chance's sister, she should really ask her. They'd talked about it a couple of times, and with the wedding coming up fast, they needed to decide and get suits and dresses made.

Carter put his fork down. "Maybe you shouldn't have a wedding party. Maybe it should be just the two of you."

Hope loved that he was so thoughtful about people's feelings. Chance had told her that Carter was the one who was always working to hold the family together as one big happy unit. Here he was, doing it again. He was wanting to make sure that no one's feelings were hurt.

Cassidy smiled. "You know I was only joking, right? I didn't think how difficult it would be for you. Chance has four guys here, and I think probably one or two in Summer Lake who he would want to be his best man and groomsmen. All of whom he's known for years and is very close to. You've got the same number of women, none of whom you've known for very long at all. That's got to be tough. I don't envy you that one, girlfriend."

Hope nodded, glad that Cassidy had brought it out into the open. "It's not easy."

"You need to do what's right for you," said Gina. "Don't worry about it. No one's going to get upset if you don't ask them."

"Except me," said Cassidy with a laugh. "You pick whoever you want, as long as I'm one of them."

Hope laughed. She liked Cassidy a lot. "Okay, glad you set me straight about that."

~ ~ ~

Hope drifted off to sleep in the truck on the way home. She didn't even wake up when Chance brought the truck to a stop in front of the cabin. He got out and went around to the passenger door. She opened her eyes and smiled.

"Sorry, I guess I'm tired."

"It's not surprising. You've been working hard." He picked her up and her arms came up around his neck. He loved the way she did that when he carried her.

Once they were inside, he took her straight to the bedroom and laid her down on the bed. He went into the bathroom, expecting her to be asleep when he came out. She wasn't. She was lying there wide-eyed, looking troubled.

"What's the matter, honey?"

She shrugged. "I can't get my mind off the whole wedding party thing. I know Cassidy was only joking, but it's been getting me down for a while. I don't know what to do, so I haven't done anything, but time's running out. I need to decide and I don't know how."

"Yeah. If it's any consolation I feel the same way. I don't know who to ask."

"It must be even harder for you."

"Nah, I think you have it the hardest. I'm a guy, they're guys. It's not such a big deal to us."

Hope sighed. "That's probably true. I can't even find a bright side on this one."

"Aww." He stroked her hair away from her face. "Why don't you get undressed and get in bed before you fall asleep like that? We can talk about it tomorrow. You're tired and you've got to be up early."

She got up and got undressed, letting her clothes fall in a pile at her feet, which wasn't like her. "I don't think I can get to sleep. It's all going around and around in my mind. I've pushed it away for too long already and now I need to find a solution. I don't avoid problems normally. I can't keep hiding from it."

"Okay, let's figure it out, then. What kind of wedding party do you want, and who would you like to be in it?"

She sighed. "I just don't know."

"Okay, let's take it back a step. Who are you even considering?"

"Well, there's Missy, of course. She should be part of it."

"I can tell you now, she won't mind one bit if you don't ask her. She cares about all that stuff about as much I do. She just wants to be there. She doesn't need to be a part of it."

"But she should be; she's your sister."

"It's not about should. It's about what you want. Who else is there?"

"Well, the four girls, and I have no idea how I'd choose between them. Should I ask all four? If I did, we'd probably end up with more people in the wedding party than people attending."

He chuckled. "You've got a point there." He'd been surprised, to say the least, that her guest list had been so much shorter than his. "So, you've got five possible candidates and what are you thinking? A maid of honor and some bridesmaids?"

She shrugged. "I don't know what to think."

"Who would be your maid of honor?"

"It has to be Missy."

"I told you. It doesn't have to be anyone. Who do you want it to be?"

She met his gaze. "Someone I haven't even mentioned yet."

He frowned, wondering if she had a friend she'd never mentioned to him. "Who?"

"Renée."

He stared at her for a long moment.

"I'm sorry. I probably shouldn't have mentioned it at all, but it's been on my mind for weeks. I like her. I feel close to her. That night at the Boathouse when we went off together to talk? She told me that she still saw you as part of her family. I told her I envy you that, you have people here and there who want you in their family. I only had my dad, and he didn't even want to be a family after Mom died. Renée said she hoped that maybe someday we'd see each other as sisters-in-law. That meant a lot to me. I want it to be that way, but I don't know if it'd be too weird for you."

Chance shook his head and swallowed around the lump in his throat. "If that's what you want, you ask her. As long as you're doing it for you and not for me."

"If anything, I wouldn't do it because of you."

"No. I love the idea. Not because of Chloe. I need you to understand that. Chloe's just a memory now. You're the woman I love. You're the one I want to spend the rest of my life with. I love the idea of you choosing Renée because it's like my whole world coming full circle. My past and my future coming together in the present. I feel like you're making me whole again. I was broken for so many years. You've put me back together and not only given me a future, but you're giving me back my past—in a new way, a healthy way. I can be friends with Renée and I can go back to the lake and be happy and have fun there. It's going to be weird, but good, to have everyone come together on our wedding day. It's my two worlds and my entire history colliding in one moment."

She put her arms around his neck and planted a kiss on his lips. "If that's how you feel, then I'm going to ask her."

He smiled. "You do it."

Hope nodded. "And I'm only going to ask her. Since I can't ask all the others, I'm not going to ask any of them."

Chance nodded. That made sense to him.

"But I feel bad about Missy."

"Don't." He grinned as an idea struck him.

"Why? What are you thinking?"

"I'm glad you don't want to ask Missy, because I do."

"What do you mean?"

"I'm in the same spot as you when it comes to a best man. I can only ask one of them, and I don't want to. If I did, it would be Mason, but it's not that easy. I was Beau's best man and maybe I should ask him. I wasn't joking when I told you Shane was my agony aunt after Oregon; part of me wants to ask him because of that. Carter would rather stay out of the limelight, but I know it'd mean a lot to him. I love them all. Since I can't have all of them, I don't want any of them." He chuckled. He couldn't help it. It was a crazy idea, but he loved it. "Would it be too weird if I asked Missy to be my best man?"

Hope squinted at him, as if trying to make sense of what he'd said. Then she grinned, too. "It wouldn't be weird at all. It'd be absolutely perfect!"

"Then that's what I'll do."

Chapter Nineteen

Chance got to the barn a little later than usual on Monday morning and was surprised to find Mason in there brushing down his horse, Storm.

"Hey," Mason greeted him with a grin. "It's not like you to be running late. Is everything okay?"

"Yeah, it's all good. Hope wanted to talk about the seating plan one last time before she went up to her dad's for the day." He blew out a sigh.

"Never mind, I know all the preparations must be getting to you, but this time next week, you'll be married. The wedding will be behind you, and the best years of life will be ahead of you."

"I know. The preparations aren't so bad; Hope's done the lion's share of it all. It's the seating plan. It finally hit me that my dad and your dad are going to come face to face for the first time."

"Isn't that a good thing?"

"It is, I want them to. I've wanted them to meet for a while now, but part of me is a bit leery about it all. My two fathers, my two sets of friends, my two sets of families." He shrugged.

"My two worlds, my past and my future. They're all going to come together on Saturday."

Mason grinned. "And it's scaring you shitless?"

Chance laughed. "Kind of. Don't get me wrong, I can't wait to marry her. I can't wait to feel as though my life is whole, instead of being divided in two halves with me hanging like a lost soul in between them; but yeah, if I'm honest, it's scary."

"That's understandable, but like I said, by this time next week, it'll all be done. The two halves of you will be one and you won't be lost anymore."

Chance smiled. "Thanks, Mase."

"No worries. I'm looking forward to it. I'm looking forward to seeing you pull it all together and finally be happy."

"And you don't mind about the best man thing?"

"Nah. I think it's awesome. I think it's the best solution you could come up with. If you'd asked any of the other guys, I think I would have been a tiny bit jealous, if I'm totally honest. I know that's dumb, because I asked Shane to be my best man. But I couldn't ask you because of Beau."

"I know, I understand that. I understood it at the time."

"I think you asking Missy is perfect. She's your sister, and I know the two of you are close. I've always wanted to meet her, and I've often thought how hard it must be on her, that you're here and not there."

"Yeah, she's never had it easy and I've carried a lot of guilt over the years that I should have been there for her. She cried when I asked her, and Miss isn't a crier."

Mason grinned. "I don't imagine she is. You did the right thing asking her. And Hope asking Renée … I know you said you're cool with it, but are you really?"

"More than okay. Renée's like family to me. She's got no family left, and I still feel like that's my fault."

Mason shook his head.

"I know, I know it's not my fault, and this isn't motivated by a negative, it's not about me making up for some guilt over the past. It's about Hope wanting to help me shape our future. She gets along with Renée. They've got their own thing going, even aside from me. It may seem weird from the outside, but to us it feels right."

"That's all that matters."

Chance nodded. "It is. Anyway, I'd better get going. I need to keep on top of things this week, since I'll be out for a couple of weeks after Thursday."

"Don't worry about it, we've got you covered. I don't want you to give this place a thought while you're gone. You have two weeks and Hope and a jet to take you wherever you want to go."

"Thanks. I'm looking forward to it. We haven't even decided what we're going to do yet, but it doesn't matter."

"Okay, well I guess I'll see you on Saturday, if I don't see you before."

"Wow, I guess so." Chance went to get Maverick from the pasture behind the barn. The realization that he might not see Mason again before his wedding day brought it home just how quickly it would be here. He smiled. He wanted a fast forward button. Everything between here and Saturday was just detail. He wanted to skip that and get on with marrying her.

~ ~ ~

Hope turned into the driveway at the Davenport Ranch and brought the Land Rover to a screeching halt. "Shit! Shit, shit, shit, shit, shit!" There were two press vans, a bunch of cars and a whole crowd of photographers standing around. She blew out a big sigh. Why? Why now?

They'd spotted the Land Rover and were surging toward her. She could either turn around and get the hell out of there or press on through. She chose the latter. She fixed her gaze straight ahead, turned the radio all the way up to drown them out and drove toward them, not slowing as they crowded around and in front of the vehicle. She went slow enough that they could get out of the way, but not so slow that they didn't have to move. She clenched her jaw and stared determinedly ahead as they shouted their questions and tapped on the windows. When she got closer to Uncle Johnny and Aunt Jean's place, she saw Brody hurrying down the driveway toward her, a shotgun over his arm. She nodded as she passed him and he nodded back, but then turned his attention to the reporters. He stopped them from following her, and when she checked the mirror, he was herding them back up the driveway. She doubted they'd give him too much of an argument.

Her aunt and uncle came out when she reached the house.

"Sorry, Hope," said Uncle Johnny. "They showed up about ten minutes ago. I have no idea what they know or why they're here now. We tried to call you to warn you."

Hope checked her phone and saw she had missed calls, but her volume was turned all the way down. "Sorry. I didn't hear them. It wouldn't have made any difference anyway. I have to see Dad. Does he know?"

"I just got off the phone with him," said Aunt Jean. "I couldn't get through to him until just now, either. We were worried when they showed up and neither of you were answering."

"Why do you think they're here?"

Uncle Johnny looked grim. "They must have found out about the wedding."

Hope nodded. It had been a stupid question, but she thought they'd been so careful. "The only people who know are family and very close friends. Dad had all the vendors sign confidentiality clauses."

"Things always leak out somehow, Hopey. You know that."

She sighed. "I do. I should have expected it, really."

"You can't let it spoil your big day," said Aunt Jean.

Hope shrugged. "I know, but I can't help feeling that they've already ruined it."

"Don't, Hope," said Uncle Johnny. "Don't be like that. You're the one who finds the bright side, remember?"

"I am usually, but this is horrible. It's bad enough for me, and I'm used to it, but Chance? He'll hate it. I know he will. Maybe we'll have to postpone it."

They looked at each other. "You can't do that," said Uncle Johnny. "You've put so much work into it already. Everything's set for Saturday. And besides, you and Chance have been so eager to get married as soon as you can so you can begin your life together. Are you really going to let the press dictate that you wait?"

Hope frowned. Now he put it like that, she didn't want to, but she didn't see what choice they had. The day just wouldn't be the same with a crowd of reporters hanging out at the bottom of the driveway. It just wouldn't. Her phone rang. It was her dad.

"Are you all right? Did you get through them okay?"

"Yeah. I'm fine. I'll be up there in a minute."

"Okay."

She hung up and gave her aunt and uncle a sad smile. "I'd better go see him."

"You do that; be sure and stop in before you leave."

Her dad was waiting for her on the front steps. He shook his head sadly when she got out of the car. "I'm sorry, Hope. I thought we were going to pull it off."

She ran up the steps and greeted him with a hug. "I did, too. I guess that was too much to ask, though, wasn't it?"

He nodded sadly. "It seems that way. What did Chance say?"

"I haven't called him." She blew out a big sigh. "I should, though, shouldn't I?"

"Yes. I don't think we want the press showing up at the Remington Ranch and catching him unawares do we?"

Hope shuddered. "No. We don't."

"You call him. I'll go and get us some lemonade. I'll be in my office when you're ready."

Hope reached up and kissed his cheek. "Thanks, Dad."

She dialed Chance's number and listened to it ring.

"Hey, honey? Is everything okay?"

"Yeah, sorry. I don't like to call you at work."

"I've told you. You can call me any time. I like it. It makes me smile."

"I don't think what I have to tell you is going to make you smile."

"Why? What's up?"

"The press is onto us."

"How? What's happened?"

"I have no idea how, but they know about the wedding. When I got up here, there was a whole crowd of them in the driveway."

"Shit!"

"That's what I said."

"Damn!" He blew out a sigh. "Why do they care? Why do they want to spoil it for us?"

"I don't know."

"What are we going to do?"

"What do you want to do? We can postpone it, if you want to."

"I don't want to! We're getting married. On Saturday. I'm sorry. I don't mean to sound mad. What do you want to do? I'm just reacting against it. They shouldn't be able to make us change our plans."

"That's what I said, but how much are we going to enjoy the day knowing they're out there—how much are our guests going to enjoy it, if they have to run the gauntlet of reporters just to get here?"

"Do you want me to come up there?"

"No. I'm fine. I don't want you to have to drive through them. I wanted to warn you in case they know where you are. They might come after you, too."

"They'd better not." She didn't like the menace in his tone. "Sorry, honey. I'm just mad. I don't mean anything by it."

"I know, but if they do find you, please, Chance ..."

"It's okay. Don't worry. I won't do anything stupid."

She nodded, feeling bad that she'd even suggested he might. "I know."

"What are you going to do?"

"I guess I'll just spend the day here with Dad, like I planned, and see what happens in the meantime. I'll call you this afternoon. And you call me if press shows up down there?"

"Okay."

"I love you, Chance. I'm sorry this is happening."

"I love you, Hope. Don't let it upset you. We'll figure something out."

She went to find her dad in his office. He gave her a grim smile. "What do you want to do?" he asked.

"Wave a magic wand and have it all go away."

"If only I could, you know I would."

She nodded. She did know that now, even though not so long ago the idea of him wanting a magic wand to fix things for her would have seemed ridiculous. She'd thought he didn't care, but now she knew just how much he did care.

"If we're going to postpone, we need to decide quickly. Chance's family and his friends are all rearranging their lives so they can come up here for Saturday."

"But you said you don't want to do that, and you shouldn't have to."

"I know, but realistically, what choice do we have?" She sighed. "I could maybe put up with it, but it wouldn't be the same, even for me. The focus would be off the wedding, and be on the press and how to avoid them instead. I don't want that. And that's just me. It's so much worse for Chance. He's such private person, it'd ruin it for him. I know it would."

Her dad nodded sadly. "I'd like to argue with you, but I can't. I know you're right. But Hopey, even if we postpone, what do you think the odds are of them not finding out again whenever you reschedule to; they're bound to."

Hope blew out a big sigh. "I know. They're like hounds—once they're on the scent of something, they're relentless. I hate that they're the ones in charge now. We either get married with them all out there harassing the guests and trying to get any photos they can. Or we change the date and will probably have to go through the same thing again anyway. I don't know what we can do that will make any difference."

"Changing the date might not make a difference, but what do you think about changing the location?"

"Where to? I wanted to get married right here. In this house." She stopped and sniffed. "I wanted to feel close to Mom."

"I know, sweetheart, but your mom hated the press with a vengeance. She'd hate for you to go through that just for her."

"I know. It's silly."

"It isn't silly. It makes sense, but maybe there's somewhere else that you'd feel close to her."

"Like where? This was our home. This was the only place I ever lived with her."

His eyebrows came down and he nodded to himself. "This might be a good idea, and it might be a really bad one. I'm just thinking out loud, so don't worry if you hate it, it's just a suggestion."

"What?" she asked impatiently. "Where else could we get married that I might feel close to Mom?"

"Summer Lake. She loved it there." He nodded and waited for her to respond.

"Wow!" Hope shook her head. "I don't know. I mean. I don't know how Chance would feel about that. He might love it, or he might hate it."

"I know, and that's important, but before you even get to thinking about him, how do you feel about it?"

She shook her head again. "It'd make sense. Chance's family is there, and his friends. They wouldn't have to come here anymore, but everyone here would have to go there."

"Forget the practicalities. How do you feel about it? My concern is that it's Chance's place. It's where he loved and lost his Chloe." He held up a hand. "And we can deal with how he feels about that later. But what I want to know is if that feels right or wrong to you, for you."

Hope let out a little laugh. "I know everyone seems to think that I'm going to be jealous of Chloe somehow, but I'm not. I don't see her, or even her memory, as competition for Chance's affection. I see her as a friend, an ally, someone who loved him, too. She was just a girl. She lost her life when she was eighteen years old. That makes me sad for her, it makes me love her. If anything, I feel like I'm taking the life and the love that she was supposed to have." She swiped at a tear that rolled down her cheek. "I think I'd like to get married in Summer Lake; it seems right to me. And knowing that it's a place Mom loved, too, that makes it more right. It's as though Mom knew something good was going to happen there."

Her dad smiled. "Okay. Now you know how you feel about it, you can see how Chance does. He might not like the idea and that's fine, but I wanted you to be clear about your own feelings before you took his into account."

"Thanks, Dad. I'll ask him. But even if he says yes, even if it's what he wants to do, do you think we can pull it off?"

He smiled. "You're talking to the great Seymour Davenport, remember. I can make anything happen—especially if it's what my little girl wants."

Hope burst into tears. He used to call her that when they lived here. She'd been his little girl until her mom died. Now she was a grown woman and he was calling her that again—and she loved it. "Thank you."

Her phone rang and she picked it up warily. It was Chance.

"Hey, are you okay?"

"I am, but Mason just called me. The press has showed up at the ranch."

"Oh, no! Don't go back there, please."

"I wasn't planning to. Maverick and I are about to cross onto your Dad's property, I'm coming to you."

She smiled. "That's the best news I've heard all day."

He chuckled. "Yeah. We've got to find the bright side in all of this, right?"

"We do, and I'm proud of you. In fact …" She decided she may as well tell him her dad's idea now. That way he'd have time to think about it while he rode up the valley. "Dad and I were just trying to find a bright side, too, and he came up with an idea that you might like, or you might hate."

"What?"

"You said you don't want to postpone, I don't either. So, if we don't want to change the date, how about we change the location?"

"To where?"

"Summer Lake."

He was quiet for a long moment.

"It doesn't matter if you don't want to. It's just a suggestion."

"Do you want to?"

"I'd like it."

"For you, or for me?"

"I know I'd like it for me. I don't know if it would be good or bad for you."

"Do you want to know the truth?"

"Always."

"That'd make me very happy."

She smiled and breathed a huge sigh of relief. "It would?"

"Yeah. I don't know about the details. We'd have to stop all of them from coming here, and get everyone from here down there. And all the hard work you and your dad have done would have been for nothing, and I don't know where we could do it there or anything, but …"

"If we both want it to happen, we can make it happen."

"Then let's do it."

Chapter Twenty

"Wake up, Hopey."

She opened her eyes and it took her a minute to remember where she was. Her dad set a mug of coffee on the nightstand and sat down on the bed with a smile. "The big day is finally here. How are you feeling?"

She smiled and sat up and held her arms out to him. He wrapped her in a hug and she breathed him in. He smelled like her childhood. "I'm happy, Dad. This is the best day of my life."

He nodded. "That's what I wanted to hear. That's how it should be. It's the way I felt the day I married your mom."

Hope nodded and buried her face in his shoulder. "I wish she were here."

"So do I, sweetheart, but I know she's smiling down on us today, and I know that coming here was the right thing to do. It feels good, your mom feels close."

Hope wiped her eyes and smiled. "It does feel good. I'm glad we came. And thank you. Thank you so much for everything you've done to make it possible."

"I told you, anything for my little girl. I missed too much of your life. I'm lucky that you let me back into it and I'll do whatever it takes to see you happy."

She chuckled. "You've certainly gone above and beyond this week." She couldn't believe how he'd pulled everything off so quickly and so smoothly. Chance had put him in touch with Ben, who ran the resort, and between them, they managed to replicate everything she'd had set up for the wedding in Montana. The ceremony would take place in the little chapel by the lake. The reception was to be held in the largest, most luxurious vacation home in the area—which Ben told them had fortuitously had a canceled booking just last week. Ben had also promised them the same menu as they'd had at home. The flowers had proved more difficult, but her dad had ended up having them flown down in a jet last night. He'd hired an extra jet to get everyone down here and had worked with Ben to find accommodation for everyone. Everything was set, as if it had been planned this way for months.

He nodded. "I've loved every minute of it." He chuckled. "I even considered retiring early so I could switch careers and become a wedding planner."

She laughed. "You should, if you enjoy it. You'd be the best in the business."

"No, I realized that most of the enjoyment came from the fact that I was doing it for you. But now it's done, we're all set. All that's left now is to get up, get on with it, and enjoy every minute of this day."

"Don't worry. I plan to."

"Good, then don't waste any of it in bed. I'll be out on the deck, bring your coffee when you're ready."

Hope smiled when he'd gone. They were so much closer now than they'd been in years, but he still wasn't comfortable seeing her in her PJs. She got up and pulled on a pair of sweat pants and a T-shirt. Her phone buzzed with a text. It was Chance.

> *Morning, honey. I don't know if we're not supposed to even talk this morning, but I just want to tell you that I love you. I miss you. And if you've got nothing better to do, I'll see you at the altar at 2pm.*

She laughed and texted him back.

> *It's a date. I'll see you there. I love you, Chancey bear.*

His reply came back a few seconds later.

> *This bear wants his honey.*

She smiled.

> *And in a few hours, he'll have her and then he'll be stuck with her for life.*

It took a while longer this time.

> *I hope we get the chance to live a very long and happy life.*

She laughed.

> *Me too. I love you. You do what you need to this morning, and I'll see you at two.*

> *Thanks, honey. Don't be late.*

She nodded and took her phone out with her onto the deck to join her dad. They were staying in the same cabin she and Chance had when they visited. Her dad looked up. "I love it here. I wish I'd listened when Anne kept asking me to move here with you. I'm sorry, Hope. Things could have been so different."

Hope shook her head. "Everything has worked out as it should. We're here now, and we're happy, that's what matters."

He sighed. "You're right. We can't change what's gone."

"Nope. All we can do is make the most of what is."

~ ~ ~

Chance put his phone back in his pocket with a smile. He'd missed Hope so much last night. If it were up to him, the spending the night before the wedding apart would have been one tradition he'd have ignored. They'd talked about it, but it was important that Hope should have that time with her dad, and he understood that. So, she was in a cabin on one side of the resort and he was in another with some of the guys. She'd told him he should do whatever he needed to do, as well. He'd hung out with the guys last night and had a few beers. It'd been weird and cool at the same time for him to see Mason chatting with Pete and Jack. Shane and Smoke had hit it off immediately. Beau and Gabe had latched onto each other and gotten deep into a conversation about real estate and taxes, of all things. The matchup that had made him smile the most had been Carter and Dan. They'd sat in a corner talking for ages, and, surprisingly enough, it was Dan who was doing most of the talking.

The guy time hadn't been what Hope meant when she'd told him to do whatever he needed, though. She'd meant he should go to the cemetery if he wanted. He'd thought he wasn't going to go. He didn't feel the same anymore. He still loved Chloe, part of him always would, but it wasn't the same now. Still, this morning he was feeling that he wanted to go. It wouldn't be right to come back here, to get married here and not acknowledge her somehow. He didn't feel guilty; he was at peace, but everyone else he loved in the world would be there today, at the little chapel by the lake where he and Chloe had thought they'd get married. He wanted to include her in some small way. He nodded to himself and went back inside.

"What's the plan?" asked Mason. "Do we want to get you fed? It's too early to get ready yet, right? Is there anything you want to do?"

Chance nodded. "There is, but it's something I need to do alone."

"Whatever you need, bro. Do you want me to come with you and wait somewhere nearby?"

Chance's eyes pricked with tears. "You know where I'm going?"

Mason sighed. "You thought I didn't?"

Chance shrugged, not trusting himself to speak.

"Are you going to be okay?"

"Yeah. I'm not tearing up about going to the cemetery; I'm tearing up because a big dumb cowboy like you knows me so well."

Mason punched his shoulder. "It takes one to know one."

Chance nodded. "Thanks for the offer, but I'll be back."

"Okay."

When he got to the cemetery, Chance smiled when he saw the fresh flowers. Of course, Renée would have been here in the last day or two. He set his own bunch down on the ground while he made room for them. He spotted the note, inside a ziplock bag taped to the headstone by the flower pot. It had his name on the front. He took it out with trembling hands, wondering what Renée might want him to read here that she couldn't tell him later.

Chance,

This is probably a weird thing to do, but you already know I'm weird. I didn't want to bring Chloe up with you today, if she wasn't already on your mind. I know you're focused on Hope and on your wedding, and that's as it should be. But if you're reading this, then I guessed right, and you had to come here today. Please, don't be sad; I've been thinking about this a lot since I met Hope. I love her. I hope the three of us will be family going forward, I really do. What I don't want is for you to feel sad anymore. I found a new way to look at things, and I hope it might help you, too. You made Chloe happy. I know it broke your heart to lose her, but her life, short as it was, was a great one because of you. You should be happy about that, you should be proud of that. The only reason your pain has been so great is because the love you and Chloe shared was so great. Focus on that. Most women won't know in a whole lifetime the kind of love Chloe knew in her few years with you. You are such a good man that you're going to be the love of two women's lives. Your life with Hope begins today, but your life with Chloe should end today, too. Let her go. Wish her farewell and never look back. That chapter of your life is over. Go ahead and start your new one.

Love,

Renée

Chance finished reading and nodded. She was right. It was time to turn the page. He picked up the flowers he'd brought. Pink carnations. He'd read about them somewhere a while back; they were supposed to mean I'll never forget you. It seemed right. Once he'd arranged them next to the others, he sat back on his heels and closed his eyes against the tears that wanted to fall.

"I've come to say goodbye, honey. I'm getting married today." He swallowed—hard, but the tears started to escape anyway. "I've come to tell you that I'm happy now and I hope you understand that I don't feel bad about that. I think you'd want me to be happy. I'm sorry I blamed you all these years. I said I couldn't be happy because of you—because you were gone. That wasn't true. I wasn't happy because I wouldn't allow myself to be. I've figured that out since I met Hope. You'd like her. I know you would. I hope you're happy, wherever you are. I hope if you meet a guy up there you won't put yourself through the same kind of stupid shit I did. I hope you know that I still love you. A part of me will always love you, but it's time for me to live my life with Hope." He nodded and stared at her headstone. He couldn't see her face anymore. All he saw was Hope, she was smiling back at him, encouraging him.

He got to his feet and stood there for a few moments longer, but it didn't feel the same. Chloe was gone, and he knew he should go, too. He backed away from the headstone and then stopped and blew her a kiss before he turned and walked away. He slowed when he spotted a figure sitting on a bench by the gate. It was Max Douglas—Gramps, as they'd all called him as kids. Emma's grandfather. He smiled when Chance got close.
"I thought I'd find you here."
"You were looking for me?"
Gramps nodded.
"Why?"
"I thought you might want to talk to someone who doesn't matter."
Chance smiled. "You matter, Gramps. You were always there for all of us. You helped me out of enough scrapes back then."
"Maybe so, but what I think doesn't matter. What I say doesn't matter. Anything that's on your mind and in your heart right now, will matter to the people who are in your everyday life. You can't speak freely to them without fear of how it will affect them. I just wanted to be around in case you wanted to get anything off your chest before you get married."
Chance went to sit down on the bench beside him. "Thanks, Gramps. I think I'm good. I came to say goodbye. I'm okay to let Chloe go. I'm okay with it."
Gramps nodded. "I'm glad to hear it, and you can dismiss me as a sentimental old fool."
"No. I think this was an awesome thing to do, and I'll never forget it. Thank you."
They sat there in silence for a few minutes until Gramps chuckled and said, "You can go anytime you like, you don't need to sit here to make me feel better because I got it wrong."

Chance met his gaze. "That's not what I'm doing. I'm plucking up the courage to talk to you about the one last thing that's bothering me."

"Ah, in that case, take your time, but don't take too long, we've both got a wedding to be at in a little while."

Chance smiled. "Yeah, I'd better get going soon, but can I ask you something?"

"Fire away."

"You were married for a long time, right?"

"Yep, a very long time and I still miss her every day."

"Does it still hurt?"

"Yeah, not like it did at first, you learn to live with it, but the pain never goes away."

Chance nodded. "Thank you."

"Do you want to explain?"

"It's just, Alice said that Hope's name is an acronym, that the letters stand for: Hold On, Pain Ends. I felt like I should be happy when I heard that, but I wasn't. It made me feel bad because my pain hasn't ended, even though I have Hope now. And more than that, I don't want the pain to end; that'd be like saying I don't care anymore and I do still care, even if it's not like it was."

Gramps smiled and grasped his shoulder. "It's okay, son. I get it. There comes a point where the pain is the only real thing you have left of them. You don't want to let it go, and you don't have to. It just doesn't rule your life anymore."

Chance nodded and stared out at the rows of headstones.

"How about this?" asked Gramps. Chance turned back to meet his gaze. "Instead of Hope meaning: Hold On, Pain Ends, how about Hold On, Pain Eases?"

Chance smiled. "That's it. That's perfect. Thanks, Gramps."

"You're welcome. I'm glad I could help." He chuckled. "I'm glad I don't have to leave here feeling like I wasted both our time."

"No, now you can leave here knowing that you just gave me the best wedding gift of them all."

"Good, because it's the only one I got you. Come on, you'd better go get dressed and get to the church."

Chapter Twenty-One

Hope smiled at Renée. "Thank you for being here with me."
"I wouldn't miss this for the world, but we'd better hurry up. You don't want to be late."
"No, I don't. I'm in a hurry to get there, get on with it and get started on our life."
"Then let's get out of here." Renée peeked out of the window. "Your dad's waiting by the limo looking all nervous. I'm sure Chance is standing in the chapel looking the same way. Let's go do this."
"Okay." Hope fingered the delicate gold chain around her neck. Her dad had given it to her this morning. She remembered her mom wearing it and it had made her cry, but they were happy tears.
At two o'clock on the dot, she stepped out of the limo and her dad came around to take her arm. "Are you ready?"
"Yes. I am."
"That's my girl." They made their way inside the chapel and she turned and hugged Renée nervously while they waited. Then the organist struck up the "Wedding Chorus," and at the sound of the first notes, Hope stepped forward eagerly and her dad chuckled. "Slow down. He'll wait, he's not going anywhere."

She took a deep breath and composed herself. He was right. She should savor every step of this walk toward the rest of her life. Chance met her gaze. He was gorgeous in his tux, and he looked so happy. When he smiled, she knew something had changed in him; he looked brighter and as if all his burdens had been lifted from his shoulders. Her heart overflowed in the knowledge that she'd helped him get there.

Missy stood by his side, beaming. She'd decided that since she was going to be best man, she should wear a tux, too, and she pulled it off amazingly. She looked stunning.

Hope could feel all the love and support coming from everyone as they stood and turned to watch her pass. Toby blew her a kiss as she passed him and she realized that he was far from alone on the bride's side of the aisle. All the Remingtons were sitting there—for her! She bit back a sob as she passed them. All she could see were smiling faces and all she could feel was love. Shane gave her the thumbs up and Gina gave her an encouraging smile. Uncle Johnny and Aunt Jean sat on the second row with all three of her cousins. Oscar, TJ, and Reid had all made it. Oscar winked at her—he'd told her he probably wouldn't make it. The front row was empty and she felt sad that her dad would sit there alone. Looking across at the other side of the aisle, her sadness turned to happiness at the sight of Frank and Dave sitting together beside Monique and Alice. That was as it should be.

They were almost there now. Her dad stopped and Chance stepped forward. She watched as the two of them held each other's gaze for a long moment, then Chance surprised her by stepping forward and hugging her dad. Tears filled her eyes as he returned the hug. He turned back and kissed her cheek and whispered, "I love you." Then, he went and took his seat.

The pastor smiled at her, then at Chance. "Are we ready?"

They both nodded, and he smiled and looked out at the congregation. "Friends and family, we are gathered here today …."

~ ~ ~

Chance couldn't take his eyes off Hope. He stood there grinning at her like an idiot. She was beautiful. She was the best person he'd ever known, and she was about to become his wife. A cough from the pews made him turn his head. He wished he hadn't. He'd been trying not to look out at the sea of faces watching them. It was as if his whole life was there watching. From Gramps who'd known him as a kid, and whose words had finally set him free this morning, right the way through to Seymour, whose hug had just told him that now they really were family.

He dared to let his gaze rest on the front row, and his smile grew even bigger. Why had he never wanted his dad and Dave to get together before? The two of them sat shoulder to shoulder, both beaming with pride—a pride they shared. As he let his gaze travel again, Ben met his eye and nodded. How many times had he told Ben, Where there's life, there's hope? Now he'd changed it around in his mind. Now he knew that where there was Hope, there was life.

He turned back to look at her. Her eyes were filled with tears and he knew why. The pastor was about to lead them through their vows. They'd said that they were going to take the traditional vows, and when the pastor turned to him, Chance nodded and spoke very clearly and deliberately.

"I, Chance Malone, take you, Hope Aurora Davenport, for my lawful wife, to have and to hold from this day forward. I promise I will love you with all that I am through better and worse, through richer and poorer, through sickness and health, for all the risings and settings of the sun, until death do us part."

She smiled as the tears streamed down her face. He'd made his point. It was his promise, the most important promise of his life.

Hope spoke just as clearly as she repeated the same words, making her promise clear. He heard Missy sniff loudly as they exchanged rings. This was it; they were finally married!

He didn't wait for the pastor to say it. He took Hope in his arms, she sank her fingers in his hair and they kissed as if they were alone out in the mountains.

"You may now…" The pastor chuckled. "Yes, that."

Chance was vaguely aware that everyone was on their feet and cheering, his past and his present, his Montana life and his California life were all merging into one—and he couldn't stop kissing Hope. She wasn't letting him go either, so he carried on, their mouths telling each other so much that words just weren't enough to convey. In that moment, he was happier than he'd ever been. He understood that life hadn't taken away his chance at happiness. Life just did its thing, and it was up to him to decide how he dealt with it. Life had brought him Hope, and Hope had brought him back to life;

Epilogue

"Do you want me to bring you out a lemonade?" called Chance. Hope was sitting out on the back porch of their new home. He loved this place, and he knew she did, too. They'd found the perfect site to build, on a parcel that straddled the border between his land and Seymour's.

"I'm fine, thanks," Hope called back. "Just bring yourself out and sit with me to watch the sun go down?"

He came out and sat beside her on the swing. "I'm glad we decided to go for a wraparound porch."

She laughed. "And you don't mind now, that we ended up with two porch swings?"

"No, I don't mind at all now. When you first suggested it, I thought you wanted the second one so we could have people over to sit and swing with us. That idea didn't appeal too much. If you'd have told me in the first place that one was to watch the sun set and the other was to watch it rise, I would have picked them up a lot sooner."

Hope nodded. "We have them now, that's all that matters."

"It is." Chance stared out at the horses grazing in the paddock behind the house. "It's hard to believe that six months ago none of this was here."

"And now look at it. The house, the paddock, the barn, the horses. We have it all."

Chance placed a hand on her stomach, and she reached up to plant a kiss on his lips. "We have it all, and the best it yet to come."

Hope laughed. "I'll remind you about that when we're up at two o'clock in the morning changing diapers."

"I won't mind." He really wouldn't. He'd spent enough sleepless nights tending to cows and calves. He couldn't wait to lose sleep because he was tending to his own child. "Have you thought any more about names?"

"Oh, yeah. I came up with one today."

He raised an eyebrow. She'd been coming up with some crazy suggestions so far.

"How about Gloria, if it's a girl?"

"Huh?"

She laughed. "I just thought that now Faith is here, we could go for Faith, Hope, and Gloria?"

Chance groaned. "It's bad enough playing with our names. I think we should leave the baby out of it."

"I know, I was only joking, and besides, it's a boy, I can tell."

"You really believe that, don't you?"

Hope nodded determinedly. "I do. I just know it. It's a boy. And don't worry, I'm not going to name him Zeus or anything else that would go with Hercules."

Chance chuckled. "You'd better not. Getting each other the horses as wedding gifts was a great idea, but if they're going to be responsible for our child having a weird name then I might have to send them back."

"You'll do no such thing, and we both know it."

"You're right."

Hope smiled. "I knew it wouldn't take you long to realize that I always am." He narrowed his eyes at her, but she just laughed. "You don't have to worry too much. Our four boys will no doubt end up with very sturdy traditional names."

"Our four boys?"

"Yep, we've both said we wouldn't mind turning out like Dave and Monique. I think that'd be awesome. We'll have four boys, raised on a ranch. They'll be the Malones of Montana. I think that sounds like quite a story—don't you?"

Chance chuckled. "Yeah, I guess it does, but stories never turn out quite how you think they will."

"I know, and just like everything else, we'll make the most of whatever happens."

"Yeah, whatever life throws at us, we'll find the bright side, right, honey?"

"Always."

;

A Note from SJ

I hope you've enjoyed the journey with Chance and Hope. As with all my characters, I'm sure we'll bump into them again in other books.

If you haven't read my other books, be sure to check out the Remington Ranch series, where you'll see Chance with his adopted family. You can get started with book one, Mason, which you can download in ebook form FREE from all the major online retailers.

If you haven't read the Summer Lake series yet, you can start that for free too. The boxed set of the first three books is available for download from the major online retailers.

If you'd like to keep in touch, there are a few options to keep up with me and my imaginary friends:

The best way is to Join up on the website for my Newsletter. Don't worry I won't bombard you! I'll let you know about upcoming releases, share a sneak peek or two and keep you in the loop for a couple of fun giveaways I have coming up :0)
You can join my readers group to chat about the books on Facebook or just browse and like my Facebook Page.

I occasionally attempt to say something in 140 characters or less(!) on Twitter

And I'm always in the process of updating my website at www.SJMcCoy.com with new book updates and even some videos. Plus, you'll find the latest news on new releases and giveaways in my blog.

> I love to hear from readers, so feel free to email me at AuthorSJMcCoy@gmail.com.. I'm better at that! :0)

I hope our paths will cross again soon. Until then, take care, and thanks for your support—you are the reason I write!

Love

SJ

PS Project Semicolon

You may have noticed that the final sentence of the story closed with a semi-colon. It isn't a typo. Project Semi Colon is a non-profit movement dedicated to presenting hope and love to those who are struggling with depression, suicide, addiction and self-injury. Project Semicolon exists to encourage, love and inspire. It's a movement I support with all my heart.

"A semicolon represents a sentence the author could have ended, but chose not to. The sentence is your life and the author is you."

- Project Semicolon

This author started writing after her son was killed in a car crash. At the time I wanted my own story to be over, instead I chose to honour a promise to my son to write my 'silly stories' someday. I chose to escape into my fictional world. I know for many who struggle with depression, suicide can appear to be the only escape. The semicolon has become a symbol of support, and hopefully a reminder – Your story isn't over yet

Also by SJ McCoy

Summer Lake Series
Love Like You've Never Been Hurt (FREE in ebook form)
Work Like You Don't Need the Money
Dance Like Nobody's Watching
Fly Like You've Never Been Grounded
Laugh Like You've Never Cried
Sing Like Nobody's Listening
Smile Like You Mean It
The Wedding Dance
Chasing Tomorrow
Dream Like Nothing's Impossible
Ride Like You've Never Fallen
Live Like There's No Tomorrow

Coming Next
We will be visiting the lake again, I promise. There are still a couple of weddings I'd like to invite you to AND there is a whole bunch of new characters who have been not-so-patiently waiting for their own stories.

Remington Ranch Series
Mason (FREE in ebook form)
Shane
Carter
Beau
Four Weddings and a Vendetta

A Chance and a Hope
Chance Encounter
Finding Hope
Give Hope a Chance

About the Author

I'm SJ, a coffee addict, lover of chocolate and drinker of good red wines. I'm a lost soul and a hopeless romantic. Reading and writing are necessary parts of who I am. Though perhaps not as necessary as coffee! I can drink coffee without writing, but I can't write without coffee.

I grew up loving romance novels, my first boyfriends were book boyfriends, but life intervened, as it tends to do, and I wandered down the paths of non-fiction for many years. My life changed completely a few years ago and I returned to Romance to find my escape.

I write 'Sweet n Steamy' stories because to me there is enough angst and darkness in real life. My favorite romances are happy escapes with a focus on fun, friendships and happily-ever-afters, just like the ones I write.

These days I live in beautiful Montana, the last best place. If I'm not reading or writing, you'll find me just down the road in the park - Yellowstone. I have deer, eagles and the occasional bear for company, and I like it that way :0)

Made in the USA
Lexington, KY
08 August 2017